Forever Now

The Barrington Billionaires

Book Six

Ruth Cardello

Author Contact
website: RuthCardello.com
email: ruthcardello@gmail.com
Facebook: Author Ruth Cardello
Twitter: RuthieCardello
Goodreads
goodreads.com/author/show/4820876.Ruth_Cardello
Bookbub
bookbub.com/authors/ruth-cardello

New York Times and *USA Today* bestselling author Ruth Cardello returns with an emotional addition to the Barrington Billionaire series. Sophie finally meets the son her sister stole from her.

Kade:

For the first thirty years of his life, Kade Thompson knew exactly who he was and where his life in Australia was going. He made tough choices he thought his family needed—even if it meant leaving behind the one woman who had his heart.

A phone call changes everything.

His American biological parents and family have tracked him down—so, who the hell are the people who raised him?

Who is he?

The Barringtons mourned for him when they thought he was dead—now they are swooping in to rescue him.

From what?

When everything Kade thought he knew about himself comes into question, he turns to the one person who has always been there for him—Annie. Part of him always knew he'd come home to her, but has too much time gone by for her to give him another chance?

Annie:

Independence and success hadn't always been her dream. When she was younger, she imagined a much different path for herself—one that included Kade Thompson and a fairytale happily ever after with him. Painfully in love, she waited for him to wake up and realize how perfect they were for each other.

She never lost faith in him. Even after he left, she was confident he would come back to her.

He never did.

So, she picked herself up, dusted her dreams off, and made a good life for herself without him.

Until he walks into her parents' pub and says he needs her.

He's not looking for a wife or a lover—so sleeping with him is definitely not a good idea. He's reeling from the changes in his life and needs the friendship they've always shared, but she needs more than to be a comfort to him.

Annie has finally moved on. She's found happiness without him. Can she be there for him and not lose herself again?

He's not Kade Thompson. He's not Kent Barrington. He's somewhere between the two, trying to figure himself out. How could they possibly find their forever now?

Copyright

Dedication

My niece, Nichole.

When I think about my parents and the kind of people they hoped we would all turn out to be, I know they are looking down and smiling at you. Our family is every bit as crazy as those Barringtons, but you weather the storm like the rock Annie is for Kade. I'm proud of the woman you've become and to be able to call myself your auntie.

Chapter One

Nine years earlier

Pleasantly buzzed, Kade Thompson put an arm around Annie Martin's shoulders and pulled her in for a long, tight bear hug. Friends since early childhood, she was an important part of why it felt so good to be home. His parents' yard was overflowing with people who'd come to celebrate his recent graduation from university, but the day was also about making decisions on how to best move forward. And for that, he needed a moment alone with Annie.

The happy expression on her face sent uncomfortable heat through him. She was his friend, his confidant, practically a sister, although he wasn't related to her. He found her attractive. Of course he did. She was beautiful. Long, wild brown curls. Blue eyes either full of laughter or an inspiring amount of grit. It would be easy to confuse the love he felt for her with something else.

He didn't have much family, but the Martins had welcomed him and his parents to this town when they'd arrived as if they were long-lost relatives. His mother had been yearning for a quieter life, a small community where people took care of each other, and they'd found it in Bright, a beautiful mountain town in Victoria, Australia. The small town was nestled at the base of Mount Buffalo Park, a four-hour drive north from the bustling city of Melbourne.

"There's something I want to talk to you about, Annie. Something important. Can we step away for a few?"

If possible, her smile widened. "Sure."

They walked in comfortable silence into his mother's flower garden. Annie sat on a stone bench while he paced in front of her. Although he'd hardly seen her since she'd had her own graduation celebration a year earlier, time away hadn't changed how comfortable he felt with her. They were the same age, but it hadn't surprised him when she'd graduated first. She'd always been a step ahead of him, serious beyond her years, with a clear vision of what she wanted. Which was why he knew she was the one he needed to discuss this with. "You know how much you mean to me."

Annie nodded, looking oddly excited and emotional.

"Graduation is a turning point in life. Everything kind of changes from here on out. We have to step up to the plate, become adults, and start planning for our future."

"Yes, we do," she said breathlessly.

He sat beside her and took one of her hands in his. "I couldn't wait until tomorrow to talk to you about something that has been on my mind for a long time." Her fingers trembled. He frowned. Was she cold? *Sick?* Upset about something he'd missed? "Everything all right?"

She smiled brightly. "Of course. Sorry. It's just so good

to see you again."

It *was* good. He'd already forgotten half the people he'd spent time with at uni, but Annie and his friends in Bright would always be home to him. The thought of building a life without them was daunting. He took a deep breath. "I'm considering expanding my father's tour company to a town in the foothills of the Wabonga Plateau Alpine National Park." His father had built Thompson Tours into a steady business that had strong local support. People came to the area, year after year, for the personalized tours he designed for them. Whether they were looking to scale the side of a mountain or sip champagne by a waterfall, his father made it happen. With a sigh, Kade closed his eyes while holding Annie's hand tightly in his own. "It would mean starting over, putting down new roots. I hate the idea of it because everyone and everything I care about is here." He opened his eyes and met her gaze. "Staying doesn't make financial sense, though. This market is tapped out. If I go to Wabonga and build our business there, we could maintain our employees here and my dad could finally retire."

"We?" Annie's eyes seemed to light up.

He nodded. "Yes, my father and I. He's not ready to retire yet, but he's getting older, and I want to do this for him. I will do this for him."

She searched his face as her eyes dimmed. "It sounds like you've already made your decision."

He tilted his head back and looked at the white, fluffy clouds making their way across the sky. "I guess I have." He sighed. "So, my question is: how do I tell my mother? You know how she worries. If she could, she'd Bubble Wrap me and keep me here forever. This won't be easy for her."

"Your mother loves you, so of course she doesn't want you to go anywhere," Annie said quietly. She withdrew her hand from his and stood. "But if this is something you need to do, she'll understand."

"I hope so." Kade stood and pocketed his hands. "I do need to do this. This might sound crazy, but I feel like there's something out there calling to me—something I need to leave Bright to find. Ridiculous, right?"

She didn't answer, but the excitement he'd sensed earlier was gone from her eyes. "No, not ridiculous."

"I knew you'd understand. If I don't do this, if I simply stay here, I'll always wonder." With a sigh of relief, he pulled Annie in for a hug. "Thanks for talking it out with me."

"You're welcome, I guess." Annie quickly stepped out of his hug. Her eyes glistened and she rubbed them as she said, "Something must have blown into my eyes."

"Let me look." There was nothing there but sadness, which was rare. Her happiness and positivity was one of the things he loved most about her. She'd never liked change, though. He gave her another hug. "Don't worry, I'll always make time for my Annie."

Chapter Two

Present day

KADE WALKED INTO The Tap House, the pub owned by Annie's family in Bright, Victoria, and called to the man behind the bar. "G'day, Harrison. Annie here?"

"G'day, mate," Harrison Martin answered with a welcoming wave before checking the time on the clock behind him. Two years younger than Kade, Annie's brother had always felt like his brother as well. "She was in earlier to see Mum, but she had a chartered flight to Melbourne 'round lunch time. We might see her again soon for dinner. You're welcome to stick around and join us." He poured their signature pale ale, a favorite of Kade's since Annie's family introduced their children, along with Kade, to the art of quality-tasting beers at their family's main business, a beer brewery. That was back when the three of them, Kade, Annie, and Harrison, had been inseparable.

Expanding his family's tour business had kept Kade busy. Visits home had become less frequent and more rushed. In the beginning, he'd sought out the Martins and his local mates, but over time, his life had begun to revolve around where he worked and his life there. He hadn't allowed himself the luxury of thinking about how much he missed his friends in Bright. He'd been determined to make a success of the expansion, and he had. Funny how one phone call from his mother had made all he'd achieved seem instantly unimportant.

"I just might. How is she?" Kade settled onto a barstool, greeting the man on his right then the couple on his left. Bright was a tourist town, but the families who lived there were a tight-knit group—many had been in the area for generations. His parents couldn't have chosen a better place to raise him.

"Annie or my mum?"

"Both." Kade took a refreshing swig of beer. After the day he'd had, he was tempted to lose himself in a keg of it, but it was probably better to have his wits about him considering what the next day had in store for him. "I saw your parents last Christmas, but Annie—damn, it's been too long since our paths have crossed." Harrison gave Kade an odd look. Or maybe he didn't. Kade was still in a state of shock, trying to get his bearings.

After pouring a beer for another patron seated at the bar, Harrison said, "Mum and Dad are same as always. Dad's on a solar kick at the factory and so proud of himself you'd think he invented the technology himself. Ma is crunching the numbers and preparing for the changeover. Their goal is zero emission."

"That's great. Mitch has been talking about wanting to do that for as long as I can remember. And Annie?"

"She's busy with her charter business. Remember her first broken-down helicopter? The one we all thought she'd sell as soon as that phase passed? Well, she has a fleet now of top-of-the-line helicopters that fly back and forth to Melbourne for some corporate bigwigs. I thought she was in it for the adventure, but now I tease her that she runs a glorified limo service. You should see her; she even has a uniform. Very serious stuff. And you? How's it going? It's been too long since we've seen you 'round."

"Snowed under with work most days. Can't complain. It's better than no business."

"I guess. Never thought I'd see more of your dad than you. He looks a little lost since he retired."

"It was time. After his health scare last year—no one wants to see him trekking up a mountain alone or as a guide. I tried to get him to stay in the office, but you can imagine how that went."

Harrison nodded and wiped a towel across the bar. "He's real proud of you, Kade. You've done all right by your parents."

"Thanks." Although they weren't meant to, Harrison's words stung. He had no idea how complicated Kade's life had recently become. Kade was no longer the hard-working son of a good man. He didn't know what he was. Two days ago, his mother had called to tell him that nothing he'd thought he knew about himself was true. His mother and father were not his biological parents. Had it been a simple case of adoption, he could have handled the revelation. No, it had to be some far-fetched story about revenge and murder. At first he'd thought it was a joke, some kind of prank even though his mother had never been one for those. Stolen from a rich family? Hidden halfway around the world until they discovered the truth? *Bullshit.* That couldn't be his story. His parents were too normal, too nice. Until that phone call, Kade would have said his parents had never lied about anything. Now he had to accept that his mother—at least—had lied about everything. A realization like that shook a man to the core. None of that, however, was a topic for the curious ears around them. "How have you been?"

"Good. Busy. Dad spends more time fishing with your father than working the bar, but I don't mind. I used to dream of moving away, but the older I get the more I can imagine raising my own family here."

"Good for you. I had no idea you were even seeing anyone."

"I'm not." Harrison took a glass from a drying rack, flipped it in the air, then filled it with water and ice. "But the unexpected happens every day."

That was for damn sure.

Harrison smiled. "Hey, while you're here, make time for a Mystic Park run." He gave his still-flat stomach a pat. "I'm getting fat without you to drag my ass down those bike trails."

"You're on." Kade was in the best physical shape of his life. Even though he had employees who could do it, Kade still guided tours through the mountains. Nothing like the workout of setting up and breaking down a mountainside picnic for city folk who could barely carry themselves up the trails. Kade savored his next gulp of ale.

Coming to see the Martins had been a good choice, particularly in the face of the craziness going on. They would be a safe harbor and sane sounding board while he figured out how to handle the next day. He had other friends, but it was Annie he needed. Sweet, sensible Annie and her easygoing family.

Just then Mitch, Annie and Harrison's father, entered and called across the room. "Well, look who wandered home. Is that Kade, or are these old eyes imagining things?"

Kade stood, turned, and greeted the older man with a back-thumping hug. "Hey, mate."

"It's good to see you, Kade. Real good. You staying for dinner?" Harrison was the spitting image of Mitch, apart from the curls. Mitch had started buzzing his hair short as soon as his hairline began to recede, but he still looked much younger than his sixty or so years. Martins aged well—Mitch joked it was all the beer. And who could argue with him? Although Mitch was a third-generation brewer, at his family's urging, he'd studied medicine at uni. He'd even opened his own general practice in Melbourne until he came home and was served a beer by his family's new accountant, Hazel, who had agreed to work the bar one night as a favor. One favor. One drink. One woman for the rest of his life. Mitch said he was in love with not only Hazel, but the idea of applying what he'd learned about medicine to the family business. That's the way the Martins lived and loved—with everything they had. They were the kindest, most loyal family Kade had ever met, and he felt lucky to have been raised alongside them.

They also made a damn convincing argument for how a good brew added to a person's quality of life.

"I'd love to if there's room at the table." Warmth filled Kade, pushing back some of the panic that had been rising within him before he'd sought out the Martins. Not everything in his life had been a lie. This was real.

"For you, Kade, always. Hazel was asking about you the other day. You kids are all so busy now; it's hard to keep up." He waved for Harrison to pour two beers then motioned for Kade to follow him to a table off to the side. Once seated, Mitch took a healthy swig then asked, "Your dad said you came back because of family issues, but he didn't say more. Anything you need?"

Kade opened his mouth to answer but instead raised his beer and downed the entire glass. Mitch's eyes rounded.

"That bad, hey?"

"I don't even know where to begin." Kade rubbed his hands roughly over his face. "It's really fucked up, Mitch. I shouldn't come and lay it at your door, but I don't know what else to do."

Mitch put a hand on Kade's shoulder. "You couldn't be more a part of my family if you'd come out of Hazel. Whatever is going on, we're here for you, mate."

Movement at the bar caught Kade's attention. *Annie.* Even dressed in a dark blue pantsuit and white shirt, he recognized her instantly. How long had it been since he'd last seen her? A year? Two? How had that happened? Her long brown hair was neatly contained in a braid. When she turned, her blue eyes widened then narrowed. Her face didn't light with the welcoming warmth he'd expected, and he tried to remember their last conversation . . . but couldn't. There'd been no fight. Nothing worth committing to memory. Their friendship had been solid until he'd moved away.

Kade stood and met her halfway. "Annie." He was about to hug her, but she put out her hand for a shake.

"Kade. Good to see you," she said in a formal tone.

"Is it?" His hand closed over hers, and he held on rather than immediately releasing it. "You don't look happy to see me."

Seeing Kade again hit Annie like a sucker punch to the kidney. Their paths hadn't crossed in years, because she had carefully arranged to be absent whenever he'd come to town. It hadn't been difficult, as the holiday seasons were busy tourist times for both of them. His trips home had been brief and easy enough to avoid.

God, he looked good—better with every year that had passed, and considering he'd been the most lusted-after hottie in high school, that said something. Part of her wanted to throw her arms around him, as she would have when they were younger, and announce without caring who heard that she'd missed him.

It wasn't his fault she'd fallen for him in second grade when she'd spilled her milk on her sandwich and he'd given her his. Ridiculous as it seemed now, she'd decided right then and there that she would marry him someday.

Early puppy love became painful adolescent longing during her teen years. It didn't help that she also loved him as a friend. He fit in with Harrison and her like the missing piece to a puzzle. They learned to swim together, camped out with and without their parents, scaled and paraglided down mountainsides shoulder to shoulder. It was one wild adventure after another when they were together. Annie had loved it but it was embarrassing to calculate how much was simply because she was with him. She wondered if he knew the reason she'd originally learned to fly a helicopter was because in her innocent young delusions she'd imagined it would be the perfect skill for a wife of his to have. Who better to rescue him or one of his clients from a mountaintop accident than the woman who loved him?

Even when they'd separated for university, she'd told herself it would be good for them. They'd grow, have time to miss each other, and he'd sweep into town with a diamond ring and the realization that he couldn't live without her.

He'd come home after he graduated, but not to propose to her. Instead, he'd excitedly shared his plans of expanding his father's tour company in another town—without her. He'd been young, enthusiastic, and determined to earn enough to provide for his parents when they were older. Hard to hate a man like that. Even harder to love him and watch him walk away.

For a long time, she'd believed he would come back for her. Every time he'd returned and not asked her to go with him had shredded another piece of her heart. On her twenty-fifth birthday, she'd gotten drunk and handed her virginity to a man she'd met via the small helicopter charter company she'd started. He not only ended up confessing later that he was married, but he'd felt so guilty about being her first that he stuck around to talk the next morning. Before she knew it, she'd spilled the story of unrequited love to him. There weren't many more humiliating moments than having that man tell her she was wrong about Kade.

"Don't waste your best years on a man who doesn't love you," he'd warned. She could have called his wife and passed on the same advice, but he'd shown Annie photos of her and their children. They'd all looked so happy. Annie lectured him instead, first about not wearing his wedding band and then for not honoring someone he claimed to love. Neither of them enjoyed the conversation much or had the ability to understand the other person's choices.

Her married *mistake* was still married two years later when she ran into him in Melbourne. When he asked if she was still waiting for the man she'd been obsessed with, she'd realized she was. Sure, she'd dated other men, even slept with a couple of them, but none had become anything serious.

None would as long as her heart belonged to Kade Thompson.

After that frightening discovery Annie decided to close him out. She poured herself into her business and put away every photo she had of him. His became the name she asked her family and friends not to utter. They understood.

Some things were not meant to be, no matter how much a person craved them. She shook off her childish idealism about what love was, and focused on appreciating what she did have: a flourishing business, good friends, and a family she adored. Life was good. Damn good. She had enough clients that she often directed the overflow to a flight school in Melbourne. In turn, several of their pilots came to work for her when they finished their training.

Although love hadn't come, she had dated a man from the city for over a year. Things with him had been easy and comfortable, but never great. When disagreements stopped leading to make-up sex, they mutually agreed it was over. Although memories of him sometimes brought a sad smile to Annie's lips, she didn't actually miss him.

A year of sleeping with him hadn't affected Annie as deeply as one handshake from Kade. He expected her to be happy to see him? Her heart ached for him. Couldn't he feel that? Every wall she'd built around her heart was in danger of crashing down, and he had no clue. If she let him, he had the power to break her heart again without ever knowing he did. No, she wasn't happy to see him.

She forced a smile as she tried to pry her hand out of his. "Sorry. It's been a long day. I just got back from dropping someone in Melbourne."

"Good, I thought it was me." He let her hand go. Relief flooded in. Then, whoosh, her whole world went upside down again when he pulled her to his chest for a hug. "I know I've been wrapped up in my life for too long, but it's so good to see you."

The ability to breathe left Annie as she stood in shocked stillness in his embrace.

"God, I needed this," he said into her hair. "I need *you*, Annie."

Annie closed her eyes and hugged him tight for a moment, blinking back tears as she did. She'd waited for him to come home and say those very words, but something told her he wasn't voicing them for the reason she'd craved. *Be smarter this time, Annie. Be strong.* She slowly pushed out of his arms.

But then concern for herself fell away when she saw the pain in his eyes. "What happened, Kade?"

He shook his head. "Harrison and your dad asked me to stay for dinner. Mind if I tell you then?"

"Of course." Annie's family had always adored Kade, just as his family had always fawned over Annie. It made sense he would turn to them for help. She took a deep breath and told herself if their roles were reversed he wouldn't turn her away. He might not love her, but he was a good man and had always been a good friend.

Her father called to them, so Annie walked with Kade to where he was seated with a fresh round of beers. She could have reminded her father she drank Chardonnay now, but she didn't. "Your mum is on her way here, then we'll all head back to the house. What do you say, Annie? You can change out of your uniform there."

Annie took a seat and downed half her beer. "Sounds great."

Kade sat beside her and raised his glass. "To good friends."

Annie and her father clinked their glasses with Kade's, which was when she took a closer look at her old friend. There were dark circles beneath Kade's eyes as if he hadn't slept the night before. What on earth had happened?

Her second guzzle of beer did nothing to alleviate the nervous churning of her stomach, especially when Kade met her gaze and winked. Her chest fluttered as it always had when he gave her that lopsided smile of his. He was genuinely happy to see her again. She finished her beer and groaned. Her torture was just beginning.

Chapter Three

A COUPLE HOURS later, seated at the Martin dinner table, Kade held a pan of lasagna for Annie to take some from before he served himself. She was quieter than he remembered, but perhaps that came with age. Thirty. How did that happen so fast?

As he watched her hold the pan for her brother, he was saddened by how much time had passed since he'd seen her last. He shouldn't have accepted she was working late or out of town. With all the technology available, how had they drifted so far apart? He should have made the effort to keep up on her life—on all of their lives.

It had taken his father's heart attack for Kade to see his time with his parents might be limited. He'd built up their touring company because he wanted to be in the financial position to make their later years comfortable, and it had shaken him to realize he might not have those years. When his father had said he was ready to retire, Kade had thought his biggest decision would be whether to continue to focus his attention on his touring company expansion too or come back and maintain their base.

None of that felt important now.

My parents.

No matter what he'd learned recently, no matter what he learned tomorrow—Pamela and Dave were his parents. But so were the two strangers in flight to meet him now. *God, this is surreal.*

He placed his utensils beside his plate without touching his food. A silence fell over the group as they seemed to sense he was ready to share what he'd come for. "Thank you for this. I received some news yesterday, and I'm trying to come to terms with it. There is no one outside this room I trust with this information. If it ever got out, it could prove to be dangerous for my parents."

Mitch put his utensils on his plate. "It won't go beyond these walls, Kade."

"I know that." Kade took a deep breath. "Yesterday I found out I was adopted. Well, it's more complicated than that, but what I know is that my birth family has been looking for me for thirty years." He swallowed hard. "And they'll be here tomorrow."

Harrison leaned in. "So, did your birth parents give you up and change their minds?"

"No." He ran his hand through his hair. "There's no easy way to say this so I'm just going to put it out there. My biological parents were on vacation in Aruba and were told I died at birth."

"No." Hazel's hands went to her heart. Her deep chestnut hair was cut in a bob that swung as she looked back and forth around the table as if trying to gauge if Kade could somehow be joking. "That's horrible."

Annie watched Kade without speaking. He'd known her long enough to know exactly what was going on behind those calm blue eyes of her. Annie wasn't the type to blurt out whatever she was thinking. She took information in, mulled it over, then shared it only after she'd carefully thought the subject through. He'd once jokingly asked her if she had an opinion on anything. She'd smiled and assured him she did, but censoring it for public consumption took time. Then she'd let him have it.

"Hang on," Harrison said. "Do you know anything about these people who say they're your parents? Weren't you on a cover of a magazine last year? How do we know they didn't see it and decide you're doing well enough that they want a piece of it?"

"I doubt they're after my money." Kade took out his phone and pulled up one of the stories he'd found about the Barringtons at a charity event in Boston. Shaking his head, he handed the phone to Harrison who whistled as he read.

"Holy shit. One of the richest families in the US? Seriously?" He looked at Mitch. "Dad, tell me I was adopted too."

"Idiot," Annie said softly and took the phone from Harrison. She studied the photo and read the article below it before swiping to more of the pages he'd found on them and reading those as well. "You certainly look like them."

Mitch waved a hand toward the phone. "Have you spoken to any of them yet?"

Kade nodded. "Earlier today I met a man who says he's

my brother. He and his fiancée located me through my mother. Mum's been upset since they arrived. Dad says he's fine, but he just found out Mum lied to him about me being hers." He fisted his hands on the table. "My parents are scared."

Annie asked, "How do you feel?"

Shaking his head, Kade said, "I don't know. Angry mostly. I couldn't have asked for a better childhood. My parents are good people. I don't know what these Barringtons want from me, but I know what I want from them. They need to stay the hell away from my parents."

Hazel looked on with compassion. "I can't imagine what you're going through, but help us understand this. Why was your biological mother told you were dead? Why would anyone do that?"

A shudder shook through him as he remembered numbly asking his mother the same thing. Her answer had only confused him more.

Annie's hand closed around one of his fists. "Tell us when you're ready to," Annie said gently.

He placed his other hand over hers. "It won't make much sense unless I share it all. Back in Aruba, my mother's brother somehow got involved in snatching me from the hospital. They replaced me with a stillborn baby who also born that day." He kept his eyes on Annie's hand, absentmindedly lacing his fingers through hers. "Mum said her brother was told to kill me, but he couldn't, so he took me to her. He told her there was a price on my head, and if he didn't return she should run. He didn't come back. He was killed along with anyone who might have known I was alive. My mum didn't know who to turn to. She thought I might be the child of a criminal or a gang. All she was sure of was I would be in danger if anyone found me. So she ran to someone she knew would take her in—my father. They'd broken up, but she knew he'd take her back. She lied and told him I was hers, a product of a relationship with an abusive man. He adopted me, or thought he did, but there's no likelihood of that being legal, and we moved to Bright." He sighed. "And here we are."

Everyone was quiet for a moment. Annie said, "That's a lot to take in all at once."

He gave her hand a squeeze and held her gaze. "There's more. The Barringtons arrive tomorrow. The parents, the siblings, their children."

Hazel took a sip of her water then said, "It all seems so far-fetched. I believe you, but it doesn't feel like it could possibly be true. I always thought it was strange that Pamela wouldn't talk about her family in Aruba, but this? No."

Mitch sat back, folded his arms across his chest, and took a moment to soak in what Kade had shared. "What do they want?"

Kade shrugged. "I hope just to get to know me. They seem excited to have found me. One even wants to marry his fiancée while they're here. It's too fucking much."

"Who's planning a wedding?" Hazel asked, shaking her head in disbelief.

"My brother's fiancée is pregnant, and they said they'd take advantage of everyone being here."

"What do you need from us?" Annie asked, and Kade was tempted to pull her into his arms and hug her for being the rock he'd known she would be.

He looked around the table instead and saw similar concerned expressions on the faces of her parents and brother then directed his request to all of them. "What the fuck am I supposed to do? I don't know these people. I wanted to tell them not to come, but Grant told me his mother—"

"Your mother too," Hazel clarified gently.

"My biological mother. I feel sorry for her, because she never accepted that I was gone. She and my twin have believed I was alive for thirty years."

"You have a twin?" Harrison interjected. "Damn, I want a twin."

"Harry, stop," his father admonished quietly.

Kade didn't mind. Harrison's humor was actually a welcome reprieve. If all was taken seriously, it was a bloody mindfuck. "Not an identical twin. Kenzi is a girl—a woman."

"Kade." Annie shook his hand to regain his attention. "When we were little you used to have a reoccurring dream about having a sister. Do you remember? We used to joke you were jealous that Harrison had me."

Kade raised a hand to his mouth as flashes from those dreams came back to him. "I did. I forgot about that."

"Now she has a name: Kenzi. You finally have a sister." Annie said it as if it were not batshit crazy beyond comprehending. For a moment he was lost in her eyes, in her calm acceptance of the situation. He'd forgotten how good it felt to simply be with her. She handed him his phone. "If you ever wanted more family, you hit the motherlode. Five brothers. Asher, Grant, Ian, Andrew and Lance." She smiled at Harrison. "I thought one was bad enough."

Harrison tossed a piece of bread at her. "Very funny."

Mitch cleared his throat. "Was Kade the name you were born with?"

Kade tore his gaze from Annie and shook his head. "No. Kent. My brother warned me they might keep accidentally calling me that name. I'm not looking forward to tomorrow. This is all new to me, but the Barringtons have both looked for me and mourned for me for thirty years. Asking for more time seems cruel."

Annie's voice was calm and full of empathy. "I can't even imagine what you must be going through."

"It doesn't feel real yet." Gratitude filled Kade as he met her eyes again. He'd been an absent friend for long enough that he didn't deserve the compassion she and her family were showing him, but he would make sure he did better from this point on. Some people came into a person's life for a season, and others were meant to be part of the whole journey. He couldn't imagine his life without the Martins in it. "I don't know how to handle tomorrow. Will the Barringtons be grateful my mother kept me safe or hate her for hiding me?"

"How do you see it?" Annie asked.

It was a question he'd asked himself several times the night before as he'd gone over the story again and again rather than sleeping. "I believe my mother hid me because she felt it was the only way to keep me safe. She'd lost her own brother to the people she was afraid would come for me. She lied to my father because she didn't want to endanger him. I wish they'd at least told me I was adopted, but it wouldn't have mattered. I have awesome parents, and with you guys as my family too, I've never wished for anything else. What could I resent about that? Although, if Mum had been honest—maybe I would have tracked them down by now. Would that have gotten me killed? Maybe. So, even if it was wrong, how could I hate someone for giving up everything to keep me safe?"

Hazel let out an audible sigh. "Imagine keeping that kind of secret for all these years. It must have eaten away at Pamela. She never said a word to me—to anyone."

Mitch nodded slowly. "It couldn't have been easy for her."

"Or for Sophie and Dale." Annie looked toward her own parents. "His biological parents, if I read their names right. What would you do if you discovered a child you'd thought dead was actually alive and well?"

"Nothing could keep me from his side," Hazel said hoarsely.

"I'd hate the woman who took my child," Mitch said, "and then I'd love her, too, if it meant he would have been dead without her. I don't envy what you're being asked to navigate, Kade. Tell us what you need, though. How can we support you through this?"

"You're doing it right now," Kade said in a low tone. "I needed to say this shit out loud to people I knew could handle it. The Barringtons arrive tomorrow morning, and I'm supposed to meet them for lunch. Grant said they rented out the Lavender Farm lodge. I'll see how tomorrow goes then decide if they should meet Mum and Dad."

"Sounds about right, mate," Mitch said with a nod of approval then picked up his utensils again. "Let's eat before it gets cold."

"Dad," Harrison interjected as he picked up his own cutlery, "can I have tomorrow off? I can be Kade's wingman. I'll scope out these Barringtons—listen in to a few side conversations—see if there's anything funky about them. A few shots of tequila and I'll have one of them spilling all their plans."

His mother smacked her son's shoulder playfully. "You are not getting Kade's family drunk."

"You should take Annie," Mitch suggested. "Annie, didn't you say you have tomorrow off? Might be good if you went with Kade. He could use a friend by his side."

Although his first instinct was to assure the Martins he could handle this on his own, as soon as he met Annie's gaze he knew he wanted her there. Annie would be his compass, his guide home if he got lost. "Annie? I'll understand if you say no. God knows, I wish there were a way I could get out of it, but will you come with me?"

ON ANY OTHER day Annie would have said she was a good person. In the silence that followed Kade's request, she felt like the most selfish, self-absorbed person on the planet. She didn't want to go. She didn't want to be dragged back into Kade's life—especially not to this depth.

Yet, how could she say no? He needed her.

She looked down, realized she was still holding his hand, and quickly broke off that contact. If she did this, she would have to remember it was for a friend—a good friend—not more than that. "Of course I'll go."

He leaned over, put an arm around her shoulders, and gave her a hug. "You have no idea how much I appreciate this. I owe you, Annie."

His smile was wide and genuine. The light in his eyes did confusing things to Annie's ability to concentrate. She frowned, shrugged off his arm, and tried to look unaffected by his touch. "It's nothing," she said then shoveled a bite of lasagna into her mouth and looked away.

When she made the mistake of looking at her brother, he wiggled his eyebrows at her. She kicked him beneath the table and sent him a message via a glare. Although he bent to rub his shin beneath the table, he didn't say anything. *Message received.*

The rest of dinner conversation was thankfully about the more mundane. Kade asked questions about the brewery. He shared stories from the life he'd made for himself in Wabonga. Harrison did hilarious impressions of people in town after several beers. Annie shared how her charter company had grown and the corporate direction she'd taken it in.

Kade cocked his head to one side when she finished. "It's hard to imagine you flying suits back and forth."

"Really?" Annie told herself not to ask, but she couldn't help it. "What do you picture me doing?"

His beautiful eyes darkened. "Remember that bush

fire—the big one when you volunteered to drop water? You took me on that run with you. Grown men were scared that day, but you took notes, fueled up, and did it. I remember thinking you were fearless—and heroic."

Annie swallowed and looked at her plate. "Not quite fearless. And I don't put out fires anymore."

"Harrison, what happened after I left? Did you stop convincing your sister to jump first and think later?" Kade joked. "Like the time we tried that tire swing we found by the lake? I wanted to climb up and make sure it was secured, but before I could you had Annie up and testing it."

Hazel gasped. "Annie, is that how you hurt your arm that summer? You told me you tripped over a root."

"More like face-planted on it," Kade said, even though Annie was waving for him to cease. "Not that it stopped her from trying it again after I retied the rope. Like I said—fearless."

Harrison shrugged. "Only because she wanted to impress you."

Annie kicked Harrison again, harder. *I've got to get out of here.* She stood. "I'm going to step outside for a minute if that's okay. I need some air."

As soon as she was outside on the veranda, Annie took a deep, fortifying breath. The lure of going back to how things were before was strong. It would be easier if Kade were an asshole or if he didn't like her. Annie bent to rest her arms on the railing and placed her head on her arms.

This was always the problem—Kade does love me, just not the way I want him to.

No. Wanted. Wanted him to. We've barely spoken since he left. My fault. It's too hard to hear about his new life—his girlfriends.

I will not go back to imagining him waking up and realizing I'm everything he's always wanted. I'm too old for that foolishness.

I won't ask myself if he's never married because he's never found anyone he cares for as much as me. Only an absolute fool would think like that after all these years.

I'm not a fool.

I refuse to be.

Chapter Four

A NNIE ALWAYS DID have a spectacular ass. Kade tried to look away from it when he stepped out onto the veranda to make sure she was okay. Bent over as she was, her blue cotton shorts rode high on legs long and lean enough to scramble any man's brain. *Stop. This is Annie.* Kade said her name and was relieved when she immediately straightened and turned to face him.

Annie would always be one of the most beautiful women he'd ever known, but he would never act upon it. Women came and went. He couldn't remember the names of most of the women he'd dated, even fucked, over the years. He was a healthy male. He liked women, and they'd always seemed to like him. It was blissfully uncomplicated because he kept it that way. Annie, though, had a special place in his heart. Fucking her, no matter how she sometimes sent his heart racing, would never be worth the risk of losing her. A friend like Annie was a treasure. He'd lost sight of that while away from her, but it was clear to him now.

His half-cocked dick would have to find relief elsewhere.

He leaned against the railing beside her. "Everything

okay?"

She folded her arms beneath her breasts then dropped them to her sides. "It just gets warm in my parents' house. The older they get the less they like it cool."

Kade studied her expression. She looked like she was holding something back, or it could be his imagination. "You don't have to come with me tomorrow if you're not comfortable going. I honestly have no idea what it will be like or how I'll feel when I meet them."

"I *want* to go, Kade." She pursed her lips and sat on the railing. "I'm actually impressed with how well you're handling this."

"How well?" he scoffed. "I'm freaking the fuck out on the inside."

She chuckled. "You're doing a good job of hiding it, anyway." Her expression turned more serious. "Of course you're freaking out, Kade. Everything you thought you knew about your life is now up in the air. I don't know what I would do if I were in your place."

"I do. You'd go tomorrow, just like I will. You'd smile. Somehow, you'd leave everyone feeling better than you found them, because that's what you do."

"I think you remember me being better than I am."

He edged closer until their shoulders touched. "No, I don't think so. You were always a good friend."

She folded her arms across herself again. "So good you forgot about me when you left."

He took her by the shoulders and turned her toward him. "Never. It wasn't like that." She tipped her face back to meet his gaze and desire cut through him, surprising him enough that he released her and stepped back. Kissing her would have been easy, but also selfish. She would not be the distraction he used to make himself feel better that night. His shoulders slumped as he replayed her words in his head. "I didn't forget you, Annie, but I did take our friendship for granted. I thought it would always be here—waiting for me. I poured myself into building my tour company. A month became a year. One year became five. I should have called. I should have made an effort to stay part of your life, but that doesn't mean I stopped caring about you." He ran his hand through his hair. "You and your family are the only things I'm sure of right now. I'm sorry if I didn't give you enough over the years for you to feel that way about me. I won't make that mistake again."

She covered her face with her hands. "Stop, Kade. Just stop, okay?"

"I don't understand."

She lowered her hands. "I'm no longer the little Annie who used to go on wild adventures with you. We both grew up, Kade. We're thirty. Not little kids. You don't have to apologize for living your life. I lived mine too."

He wiped a tear from her cheek, hating that he was the reason for it. This wasn't the strong, ever-optimistic Annie he'd grown up with. "Then why are you upset?"

She pulled back from his touch, blinked a few times, then squared her shoulders. "Maybe it's time you know. Kade, I—"

Harrison burst onto the veranda. "Mum said we are not

having dessert until you two fools are back at the table. Could we hurry this along?"

"Tell her we'll be right there," Kade said before instantly turning back to Annie. "What were you about to say, Annie? What do I need to know?"

Her eyes shone with tears that she contained. She opened her mouth then closed it as if she'd changed her mind about saying something. She touched his arm. "Just that I could have been a better friend to you, as well. I'll also try harder from now on."

He pulled her to him and kissed her forehead. "Good, because I need you at my side tomorrow. Five brothers and a twin sister, Annie. Holy shit." She fit against him as naturally as if they were a longtime couple. "Who should I tell them you are?"

She shuddered against him, sending another wave of confusing feelings through him. "Tell them the truth. We're just really good friends."

He hugged her tighter for a moment then released her. "We should probably go in before Harrison comes out and throws dessert at us."

Annie laughed. "He only did that once. Do you remember? We both chased him down and doused him with the hose until Dad pulled us off him."

Kade chuckled. "He deserved it. He got icing all over your face."

"We were older. We probably could have handled it better."

Their eyes met and they both laughed and said in

unison, "Nah."

Kade offered his arm to her. She accepted it, looping hers through his. Together they walked back into the house.

LATER THAT NIGHT, after Kade left, Annie went into her parents' attic and pulled out a box she hadn't had the heart to throw away but had needed to separate herself from. She was carrying it out to her car when Harrison met her in the driveway.

"Annie, sorry about dinner. I was just having fun with you."

She hugged the box to her chest. "I know. Sorry about your shin."

He opened the boot of her car for her. "What's in the box?"

"Just old photos and junk. Seeing Kade again reminded me it was still here. I thought it was time to help Mum and Dad declutter."

After slamming the trunk closed, Harrison leaned against it. "Is it still hard to see him?"

Fuck yes. Annie shook her head. "No. It was actually really nice. Sure, I had a crush on him, but we were also friends, and that's what was there today."

He arched an eyebrow. "And nothing else?"

She shrugged, hoping it was convincing. "Nothing beyond a real sympathy for what he's going through. It can't be easy to hear what he heard. He meets his biological family tomorrow. Can you imagine that? He must feel so lost."

"Lost enough to come here."

"Because he knows we care about him."

"And we do." Harrison straightened. "But Annie . . ."

Annie opened the driver's door to her car and glanced over her shoulder at Harrison. "Yes?"

"Don't let him hurt you again."

Annie grimaced. "He never hurt me, Harry. I did that to myself. Luckily, we're all older and wiser, right?"

Harrison nodded.

Annie closed the door, waved one last time, and drove off. She kept her mind occupied by listing the errands she'd planned for the next day but would need to postpone. It wasn't until she was seated in the living room of her apartment that she let herself remember how good it had felt to be in Kade's arms.

She opened the box she'd taken from her parents' attic and began to flip through the loose photos inside. A younger Kade was right there beside her during all the big moments in her earlier life. A photo of them when they were ten, dirty as two pigs who'd just rolled in mud. She couldn't remember what they'd done that day, but it must have been fun. Another photo of them in high school, posing with their dates and then together. Her feelings for him were right there on her face as she smiled at him and hung on his arm. She felt bad for her date. He'd never stood a chance.

Finally, she came across a photo from the day Kade had mentioned, the day they'd volunteered to drop water on a local brush fire. She was standing tall and proud at his side, all smiles and just as brave as he remembered—because he was at her side.

She vowed then to volunteer again for search and rescue. Somehow she'd left that behind along with everything else that had reminded her of him, like sitting around sharing a beer with her dad and Kade.

She held Kade's photo to her chest. *I did so much with you that I wouldn't have done had I never met you. I'm a stronger, happier person today because you were in my life. That's what I will hold in my heart. That's what I'll use to make a real friendship with you possible.*

She took the photo with her and placed it beside her bed. *I hope I can somehow make tomorrow easier for you.* Then she took a hot shower and had an hour of tossing and turning before the blissful escape of sleep.

Morning came to her much as Kade had, full on, whether she was ready for it or not.

Chapter Five

Although Annie hadn't spent time with Kade in years, conversation had never been difficult between them. Seated beside him in his Ford Ranger, Annie had no idea what to say. In silence, they drove outside the town toward the lodge his biological family had rented. She didn't want to chatter on, not when his hands were already clenched on the steering wheel and his distant expression said he was a million miles away from her. He'd hardly said two words to her since he'd picked her up.

Did he change his mind? Is he wishing he could face his family alone? How do I ask him that without sounding like I don't want to meet them?

As if he could sense her thoughts, he reached over and took one of her hands in his. "Thank you for coming with me, Annie."

Her fingers laced through his. "You're welcome." He was a simple man, a grateful man. She'd dated men who showered her with flowers, some who made promises they had no intention of keeping. Not Kade. He said what he felt. They might have drifted apart, but she believed him when he said he had never stopped caring about her. In some ways it made being with him more difficult. How could she keep her heart closed to a man if she couldn't hate him? Couldn't even be angry with him?

"They rented the whole lodge. Thirty rooms." His hands tightened on hers, and he pulled onto the side of the road and turned toward her. There was so much emotion in his eyes, and she wanted nothing more than to unclip her seat belt and fling herself in his arms. But that wasn't what he wanted.

Or was it?

Time suspended as they looked into each other's eyes. Everything around them faded away until all that existed was him and how good her hand felt in his. "Annie—"

"Yes?"

"This feels wrong."

Which part? Unless she was completely delusional, he was about to kiss her.

That would be wrong—and so, so right.

He growled and hit his steering wheel with his free hand. "Grant called me this morning. He said Sophie—my biological mother—received therapy for years because she remembered holding me before I was taken. Everyone told her she'd imagined it, and because of that she's been emotionally fragile since. She was the one who kept pushing for them to look for me. He said he's worried how she'll handle meeting me and asked me not to correct her if she calls me Kent. I'm not Kent. I don't want to be Kent. They might have been looking for me all this time, but I haven't been looking for them. Seeing them, going by another name, feels disloyal to my mother—my real mother—the one who gave up her life to relocate and save mine. I don't want to meet them today. I want to turn around and go home."

"Of course you don't want to go." Guilt washed over her. *I am horrible, foolish, and still imagining something that is clearly not there.* She looked at their linked hands then back to meet his gaze. *Get your shit together, Annie. Just friends. And he needs you.* "That's normal. You love the mother who raised you. You don't even know this Sophie, and it feels disloyal to meet her, doesn't it?"

Kade nodded. "What if they see my mother as a criminal? God, she won't even kill flies—she herds them out of the house instead. She's trying to find homes for puppies from a pregnant stray dog she took in."

"Pamela is amazing."

"She looked scared when I left the house this morning, Annie. I told her everything would be okay, but I don't know that. The Barringtons are rich. She's worried they'll want to prosecute her for kidnapping me." He slammed his hand onto the steering wheel again. "I won't let that happen."

"Maybe it won't be like that." A memory from the night of his graduation party came back to her. "Kade, when you left Bright, you told me it was because you felt there was something out there that was calling to you. What if a part of you knew there was a family out there looking for you? This might be what you've been seeking."

He frowned. "How do you remember everything I've

said?"

"It's a gift," she said lightly. *Or a curse.* "Listen, I don't believe the Barringtons would come all this way—bringing their children—planning a wedding—to cause trouble. I bet they're going to hug you too long, cry more than you're comfortable with, and hate to go back to Boston without you. They're here to meet you and put their sadness over losing you behind them." *The same way I have to.* "Give them a chance. I bet you end up glad they came into your life." *Just like I am determined to be.*

He brought her hand to his cheek and closed his eyes briefly. "That's a version of this I can handle. Annie, what would I do without you?" With that, he dropped her hand and pulled the car back onto the road. *You'd do what you've done for years without me.*

"YOU'D SURVIVE." SHE laughed, because if she didn't she'd cry. Part of her wanted to tell him this was too hard for her. She wasn't strong enough to be this close and not be more to him.

He glanced her way and smiled. "Thankfully I have no plans of testing that theory. No matter how today turns out, I want you to know I won't be a stranger anymore. I've missed you, Annie, and I'm going to make sure it doesn't take something like this to get us together again."

Annie swallowed hard and looked out the window without answering him. He wasn't the problem, never had been. *It has always been me.*

And this stupid heart of mine that doesn't understand when to give up.

KADE FLEXED HIS hands on the steering wheel as he pulled onto a long dirt road that led to Lavender Farm and the lodge the Barringtons were gathered in. He glanced at Annie again and love for her swept through him. She could easily have told him the bond they'd once had was gone and she wished him well but didn't want to be pulled into what was sure to be an emotional scene. Another woman might have been nervously preening and making the situation even more stressful. Not Annie. She was a rock of strength and support.

"Kade, look out," Annie said urgently, pointing ahead of them.

Kade's attention whipped back to the road where two jean-clad men were walking toward them. He slammed on his brakes, coming to a sliding stop a few feet before them. Neither looked bothered. As they approached the car, Kade tried to match their faces with the photos he'd seen of his brothers. If they were relatives of his, they didn't fit his expectation. They were built like Nordic woodsmen, tanned as if they spent their time outdoors, and rough like they knew their way around a bar fight. One knocked on his car window. Kade opened the window.

"You Kent?" one asked.

The second man punched the first in the arm. "Idiot, we're supposed to call him Kade. His birth name might make him go wacko or something. Remember what Viviana said? Think."

"You think." The first man rubbed his arm, then shoved

the second man back. "You don't tell a man who might go wacko that you think he will. What the fuck is wrong with you?"

"I think I know these two," Kade said to Annie before he pushed his door open. "Any chance you're Connor and Dylan, Grant's future brothers-in-law?"

They both beamed smiles at him. One held out a beefy hand. "I'm Dylan. And this jackass is my brother, Connor. Viviana's brothers. Holy shit, you look like a Barrington . . . but normal."

"Thank you?" While Kade shook their hands he heard the passenger door open and close. Annie was beside him, introducing herself to them as well.

When she shook Dylan's hand he held on a moment too long and asked, "Can you say something again? I might just be in love."

Connor shook his head and socked his brother in the arm, an act that instantly released Annie's hand from Dylan's. "Sorry, Annie. We don't let him out much. Not getting laid on a regular basis has affected his brain."

"I'm going to affect *your* brain," Dylan growled at Connor then he turned to Annie. "I get laid plenty."

Kade's eyes flew to Annie's to check her reaction. If they were upsetting her, he'd set the two clowns straight—even if he got his ass kicked doing it. What God had slighted them on tact and intelligence, he'd made up for with sheer muscle. Annie was laughing, though, reminding him that she'd always been one who could take care of herself.

Still, it wouldn't hurt to clarify things for these two.

Kade put his arm around Annie's waist. "We're heading to the lodge. Would the two of you like a ride?"

Dylan shuddered. "No thanks. When Viviana asked us if we wanted to come to Australia we didn't picture a lavender farm with tea rooms and people trying to put napkins on my lap. If I don't know you, keep your damn hands off my crotch."

Connor laughed. "That attitude is why you don't get much action."

Dylan leaned in aggressively.

Connor stepped back and put his hands up. "Dylan's tense. He'll relax once he has a beer and talks to people a little less uptight than your family—no offense."

"Is there a bar anywhere around here?" Dylan asked Kade.

Annie thumbed over her shoulder toward the way they'd come. "The best beer is at my family's pub in Bright. If you tell Harrison I sent you, you'll get a round for free—maybe two if you laugh at his jokes." She gave them the address of the bar.

Dylan's hands went to his heart and he turned to his brother. "Her family owns a brewery. I've met my perfect match."

Connor tapped his own forehead. "He's not the brightest. Dylan, Annie is with Kade."

Dylan wiggled his eyebrows at Annie. "People break up. Just keep me in mind."

"I'll do that," Annie said with a laugh and a wink.

"We need to get to the lodge," Kade said with more irritation in his voice than he'd meant. Even though the idea of Annie with either of those men was ludicrous, he held her a little tighter to his side. He'd never imagined Annie with another man and now that he had, he realized he didn't like it one bit.

"It was nice to meet you both," Annie said, still looking more amused than Kade felt. He guided her to the passenger side of the car and opened the door for her. Once she was back inside he turned back toward Connor and Dylan.

They flanked him as he walked to the driver side. Kade looked back and forth between them. "I'm sure we'll see each other again."

Connor's expression turned serious. "Hey, Kade . . . Kent . . . do you really care what we call you?"

Dylan interjected, "Do you have a nickname like— Buddy?"

"No. No, I don't. Call me Kade," Kade said.

"*Kade*," Connor leaned in and lowered his tone. When he spoke he sounded earnest. "If Viviana asks, tell her we were on our best behavior. This is her wedding trip, and we promised."

Dylan rocked back on his heels. "She'll kick our asses if she thinks I was coming on to your girlfriend. I was just having fun. I would never make a move on Annie. Nope. Not unless you were way, way broken up. I mean, like totally over."

There was no way he was about to tell either of them that he and Annie were just friends. "No problem. But, just so we're clear"—Kade slugged Dylan in the arm as hard as he could. Fuck, it was like punching a wall, and the bastard smiled—"Annie's mine."

Dylan turned to his brother. "I like this guy. He might be my favorite Barrington." Kade almost denied that he was one but let it drop.

Connor nodded in approval. "Can we walk to that bar?"

Kade shook his head. "You'll need a car. Do you want a ride?"

"Nah." Connor motioned toward himself and then toward Dylan. "With our good looks and personality? Don't worry about us. We'll hitch a ride there and be back before you two are done with your tea and scones. What the fuck is a scone anyway? Is it a biscuit? Is it a cookie? Call it what it is."

"Well, good luck." Kade shook his head and climbed back into his car. Only once Dylan and Connor had walked off did Kade shake his hand and inspect his reddened knuckles.

Annie touched his arm. "What was that about?" she asked while nodding toward his knuckles.

Mine. That's what he'd called her and it had felt right too. Pain forgotten, Kade looked into Annie's eyes and fought a primal impulse to pull her to him and lay his claim to her with a kiss. He shook his head and blamed the craziness of the day for the confusing feelings surging within him. Was she seeing anyone? Who was he? Did he make her happy? Did she cry out his name when they fucked?

Kade's cock twitched to attention even as he fought against imagining Annie naked and shuddering beneath him as she climaxed and he pounded into her. He'd never let himself imagine her that way, and it bothered him that he hated every man who had ever touched her.

Who had been her first?

Her last?

His mood took a downward turn as he wondered if the day would end with her going home to another man. *Fuck.* He started the car, writing off those feelings as too dangerous to introduce to an already crazy day. He pulled back onto the road and said, "It's a guy thing."

Annie rolled her eyes. "I realize you haven't asked my opinion, but for what it's worth I think today will go better if you keep the number of people you punch to a minimum."

"You think?" Kade asked then chuckled and relaxed. She'd always been able to make him laugh. He was still fighting a stronger than normal attraction to her, and it frustrated him. When the dust settled, all that mattered was keeping the people he loved safe—Annie included. "I'll try."

His mood switched gears again as the road opened to the lodge's large driveway. Grant was on the porch with an older woman with white hair dressed in a beautiful flower-print dress. At the sound of their car approaching, the two turned and waved. Every muscle in Kade's body clenched painfully. He tried to breathe but couldn't. He wasn't used to fear. Hell, he was the first to jump out of a plane, the one who led the way for others down unknown paths. He had faced wild animals without ever experiencing this rush of adrenaline.

This was an entirely different adversary—this meeting.

These people held the very fabric of his life in their hands. How would he feel toward them after today? Toward himself?

He parked the Ranger and sat there for a moment. Nothing would ever be the same. There was no turning back the clock. No matter what he wanted the truth to be, the man on the porch was his brother and the stranger beside him was likely his biological mother. Just as he had faced his father's health issues—he would face this.

Annie pried one of his hands from the steering wheel and held it between both of hers. "You've got this, Kade."

He brought her hands to his lips, kissed one on the knuckles, then met her gaze. "Holy fuck, Annie, I didn't think this would be so hard."

Her eyes teared up. "Me, either, but everything is going to be okay. I'll be right there with you."

He gave her hands a final squeeze then unbuckled his seat belt and went around to open her door. Her hand slid into his and stayed there as if they were the couple Connor thought they were. Kade didn't ask himself why, he was just grateful as hell to have her beside him as he walked toward the lodge.

The older woman said something to Grant then rushed down the steps, meeting Kade and Annie at the bottom of them. With tears filling her eyes and her hands clasped in front of her, she said, "Look at you. My baby." She wiped a tear away from one of her cheeks. "It really is you."

She put out her arms. Kade gripped Annie's hand tight and stood there, frozen. The woman's expression fell and she swayed. Grant was at her side in a flash. He studied their mother's face then Kade's.

In a calm, even tone, Grant said, "Kade, we're so glad you came. I can imagine this isn't easy for you. It isn't for us either, but we'll muddle through somehow." He turned his attention to Annie. "And this is?"

Without looking away from his mother's face, he said, "My friend Annie."

"Welcome, Annie. My name is Grant. It's a pleasure to meet you," Grant said smoothly.

"Thank you," Annie said. "It's so nice to meet you too. And you, Mrs. Barrington."

"Call me Sophie," the woman said, looking as if she was fighting off a fresh bout of tears while bringing a shaking hand to her mouth. "I'm sorry, I told myself I would do this so much better."

"You're doing fine," Kade said in a strangled voice.

Sophie stepped closer and raised a hand to Kade's face. He forced himself to stand and accept the touch. "You have Asher's chin and Andrew's hair. Those ears are definitely your father's. Grant, you found him. I still can't believe you found Kent."

Kade turned his face away and stepped back.

Grant placed a hand on his mother's shoulder. "Believe it, Mom. It's really him."

Sophie looked from Grant to Kade then said, "Grant, go in and tell everyone he's here, but please give me a moment alone with him."

Although Grant didn't look like he wanted to agree, he

nodded. "I'll be right back—"

Sophie patted Grant's arm. "I'm fine, Grant. There are just a few things I want to say to Kent before he meets everyone."

"Would you like to come with me, Annie?" Grant asked.

Annie looked at Kade and cocked her head in question. He didn't want her to leave, but he didn't want to say it in front of Sophie. Things were already uncomfortable enough.

There was such compassion and understanding in Annie's eyes, he knew he would never forget this moment. No one ever had or ever would understand him the way she did. She turned and smiled at Grant. "If it's okay, I'll stay here."

Sophie gave Annie a warm, approving look. "That's fine."

Grant turned and walked up the steps, disappearing into the lodge.

Kade held Sophie's emotionally charged gaze. Part of him wished he knew how to comfort her. Another part wanted to retreat from her and the upheaval she had brought with her. He held his breath and waited for her to speak.

Chapter Six

WATCHING KADE WITH his mother was heartbreaking. Annie had never seen Kade so unsure of how to handle a situation. His grip on her hand was painfully tight, but she wasn't about to complain. Although she'd thought he looked like his brothers, she also saw some of Sophie in Kade as well. He had her eyes.

"I'm sorry if I'm making this more awkward," Sophie said softly. "I just have to get something out before you meet everyone."

"Okay," Kade said slowly.

Sophie let out a shaky breath. "Finding you is a miracle I'd almost given up hope on, and we are all so happy, but it has also been hard on some of the family. Especially your father."

My father? Oh, she means Dale.

Annie asked, "Is he okay?"

"Yes and no," Sophie said. "I don't know how much I should say, but I thought I should prepare you."

"Prepare me?" Kade asked.

Sophie hugged her arms around herself. "He might be

fine."

Kade's face tightened with emotion. "I don't understand."

Tears returned to Sophie's eyes. "Just remember no matter what else you hear, what happened was my fault."

Annie's own eyes teared up. Sophie's pain was palpable.

Kade had never looked so lost for what to say.

His mother continued, "It was my sister who tried to have you killed—out of sheer jealousy. I knew she was dangerous, but I didn't want to acknowledge it. I wanted to leave my heart open to her, and you paid the price for that. I should have protected my family from her and I didn't." Tears began to pour down her cheeks again. "I am so sorry, Kent. You will never know how sorry I am."

It was a difficult scene to watch. Both of them were hurting. And confused. Annie wanted to gently correct Sophie each time she called Kade by a name he'd never known, but the woman wasn't being malicious. Annie wanted to nudge Kade to say something—but she had no idea what she would say if she were him.

Watching his mother's reaction, Kade shuddered and said, "Don't cry, Sophie. Please don't cry."

Annie blinked back tears of her own.

"Was your life here good?" Sophie wiped her face, looking at her son with wide, tormented eyes.

With her free hand, Annie touched Kade's arm. "She needs to hear it, Kade."

He nodded. "It was. I had no idea I was adopted—or *stolen.*"

When Sophie looked like she needed more, he continued, "My parents are good people. My uncle took me to my mum and told her that there was a price on my head. He warned her to run if he didn't return. She gave up everything to save me, to keep me safe. She came here to my dad. Although he didn't know the details of what had happened, he raised me as his own. I couldn't have asked for a better childhood."

"You have no idea what comfort that brings me." Sophie dried her eyes, but she was still shaking. "Do you—do you think you'll also be able to see me as your mother?"

It wasn't a fair question, and it came far too soon for Kade to handle well. He took a physical step back and Sophie's face went white.

Normally, Annie would not insert herself into such an intimate exchange, but there was nothing normal about this situation. "Sophie, Kade just found out he was adopted. He's in shock."

Sophie searched her son's face in desperation. "Tell me what you need, Kent"—her hand flew to her mouth, and she looked horrified as she corrected herself—"*Kade*. I'm so sorry. I told myself to call you Kade and I haven't yet. I'm trying. Tell me how to make this easier for you, Kade. All I want is to be part of your life."

Kade stood silent and motionless. Annie knew if he had the answers she sought he wouldn't hold them back. There wasn't a spiteful bone in Kade's body. He was as lost on the inside as he looked on the outside. After a long pause, he said, "You can be on one condition."

"Anything," Sophie promised.

There was steel in Kade's voice that Annie hadn't expected to hear. "Stay away from my parents. No one questions them. No one threatens them. I wouldn't be here today if it weren't for my mother. To me, she's a hero. You want a relationship with me, you treat her as nothing less than that."

Nothing about Sophie was threatening. Kade's reaction seemed in discord with her welcome, but it was impossible to judge Kade for feeling protective of the people who'd raised him.

"We would never—" Sophie stopped. "Grant told me what he said to Pamela when he found her, but that was before he knew the whole story. No one will speak to her that way again. She kept my baby safe, so how could I be anything but grateful to her?"

He dropped Annie's hand and walked to the car as if he were leaving.

An uncomfortable silence followed. Annie met Sophie's gaze. Her heart went out to the woman. "Sophie, he needs time. He's brave, loyal, hardworking. The Thompsons raised him to be a good man who believes strongly in taking care of his family, and Pamela and Dave are that to him. I know this must be hard for you. You finally found your son, and you want to be close to him—but you'll have to give him time to *find you*."

"You're right." Sophie blinked a few times quickly. "You are a very wise young woman. My son is lucky to have you in his life." She looked at Annie's left hand.

"We're just friends," Annie admitted hastily.

Sophie gave the area beneath her eyes a light pat. "That's the best place to start."

Kade returned and said gruffly, "Sorry." He rubbed a hand roughly over his forehead. "I needed a moment."

"Are you hurt?" Sophie asked, referencing his red knuckles. "What happened?"

Kade glanced at his hand. "Nothing."

Annie smiled. "We met Viviana's brothers."

Sophie's expression lightened and a twinkle of humor lit her eyes. "Connor and Dylan. Asher's knuckles looked the same after he met them. Boys."

Kade looked surprised at her amusement.

She glanced over her shoulder to where Grant was waiting for them. "Everyone is probably anxious to meet you. Do you have luggage to bring in?"

"No," Kade said. "We're not staying."

"I understand," Sophie said slowly. Annie was relieved to see Sophie easing the pressure on Kade. "Why don't we have everyone go out on the back deck and pool area? I'll have some food brought out. We'll make it casual so you don't have to meet everyone all at once."

"Sounds good," Kade said.

Sophie turned and began to lead the way. Kade fell into step beside Annie.

"Annie, thank you," Kade said, holding out his hand to her. "I don't fucking know what I'm doing."

She took his hand, lacing her fingers through his. "You're doing great, Kade, but stop thanking me. You would do this for me."

Chapter Seven

KADE AND ANNIE had just stepped onto the veranda when a much younger brunette came rushing out of the door with a stern-looking man on her heels. She said something quickly to Sophie then flew past her. Sophie waved to Kade and disappeared into the lodge.

There was little time to brace himself before Kade received a bone-crushing hug from a woman half his size. Still holding on to Annie's hand, Kade righted himself, then gave the woman's back a pat. She hung on, and before she said anything he knew exactly who she was. It might have been the photos he'd looked over, but he knew her. "Kenzi."

She raised her head, all tears and smiles. "Hey twin. I've missed you." She stepped back and wiped the tears from her cheeks. "I always knew you were alive. It may sound crazy, but I *felt* you."

Her simple greeting reverberated through him. He'd somehow always known about her. He glanced at Annie before saying, "Not crazy. I always knew there was something calling to me. I didn't know it was a someone."

A tall man in a dark gray suit joined them. Although he

had an imposing presence, Kenzi slid beneath his arm and hugged him as if he were a teddy bear. "This is my husband. Dax, did you hear what he said?"

"I did." He gave his wife an indulgent smile then offered his hand for a shake. "Dax Marshall."

Kade shook his hand. "Kade Thompson." It felt important to state that right away.

Kenzi exchanged a look with Dax then turned her attention to Annie. "I didn't realize Kade was bringing someone with him. Welcome."

"Thank you. My name is Annie Martin. Kade and I grew up together." She smiled warmly at Kenzi and Dax, shaking both of their hands with a naturalness that eased some of the tension. "It's a pleasure to meet more of his family."

Kade's breath caught in his throat. Not only had she validated his life in Australia—something he was just beginning to understand he needed—but she was also suggesting he wouldn't have to choose between his two families. *More family* didn't sound as threatening as what some might have called his *real family*. Pamela and Dave would always be his parents. He didn't know what these people would be to him, but Annie was a calming force. He wanted to believe something good would come from meeting with the Barringtons. However, if opening his life to the Barringtons endangered the people he loved, he would never forgive himself for not protecting them.

Breaking the silence that followed, Dax asked, "How are you holding up, Kade? You just had a bomb dropped on you."

"I'll admit it's . . . it's . . . a bit overwhelming." Kade looked past Dax, half expecting the rest of the Barringtons to charge out onto the veranda.

"Mom said she'll gather everyone by the pool. You met Grant and Viviana already. Are you okay with meeting everyone else en masse?" Kenzi asked.

Like I have much of a choice? "Yeah, I'm good."

Annie gave Kade's hand a supportive squeeze. "How many of your family came?"

Kenzi counted them off on her fingers. "Well, Mom and Dad, of course. Grant, Viviana, her brothers, and her father. Then there's Ian, Asher and Emily, oh, and their little one, Joseph. Lance and Willa brought their two, Wendy and Laney. Andrew is here with Helene and her parents." Kenzi smiled at Dax. "Oh, and we can't forget Clay and Lexi. Clay is Dax's friend and Lexi is Willa's twin sister. There were more who wanted to come, but we thought we should keep it simple."

"Simple," Kade repeated, his head spinning.

Dax nodded toward the lodge. "Your family takes a little getting used to, but they're good people."

Kenzi swatted him lightly. "Dax, that's so—"

"True?" With a smile, Dax kissed his wife on the temple. "Sorry, Kenzi. I'm flashing back to the first time I met your family. This might be different, but Kade needs to know that some of them deal with change better than others."

"They're all happy we found you, Kade," Kenzi protested.

"They are," Dax agreed, but when he met Kade's gaze, he

added, "but not all of your brothers may demonstrate that in the same manner."

Tipping her head back, Kenzi challenged, "You make them sound so . . . so . . ."

Dax didn't say anything but he arched both of his eyebrows and shrugged.

Kenzi's eyes narrowed, then a slow smile spread across her face. "*Lance* is a sweetheart."

With a grin, Dax hugged his wife. "I'll concede Lance, but the rest of them take skill to navigate. I'm just saying, Kade, if you need me, I have your back." He snapped his fingers. "I should also apologize ahead of time for my friend, Clay. He's definitely an asshole, but he really wanted to come. Give him a chance. He's a good one to have in your corner, and he'll grow on you."

"I'll keep that in mind, thanks." Kade met Annie's eyes. *What the hell are we walking into?*

Her answering smile was bright and forced.

Yeah, that's what I thought. This has the potential of being a real shitfest.

Right then, Kade added a silent caveat to how long he and Annie would stay that day. Bringing her had been an instinctive but selfish decision. If anyone was less than welcoming to her, he didn't give a shit—he'd take Annie out of there. She had been nothing but good to him and no one would mistreat her.

Kenzi rolled her eyes skyward, but she was smiling. "Now that we've practically scared you off, Kade, why don't we go in?"

Kade leaned down. "You good, Annie?"

She held his gaze for a long moment. "Let's do this."

If Kade had hoped for a moment to assess the group before they noticed his arrival, it was an opportunity that wasn't meant to be. As soon as he and Annie stepped into the pool area, conversations ended. He told himself he would probably react the same way if their positions were reversed, but that didn't make their sustained attention less awkward. Kenzi and Dax walked in first and stood off to the side with Sophie and her husband, Dale.

My biological father.

Feeling nothing beyond wishing he'd wake up and discover none of this was real, Kade forced himself to continue to walk forward. He waved awkwardly at the group in general. They waved back.

Sophie touched her husband's arm and the two of them walked to greet him. She must have asked everyone to give them a moment alone, because no one else moved. Dale Barrington didn't look as happy to have found his biological son as Sophie had been.

"Thank you for coming out to meet us," Dale said in a stilted tone. He met Kade's gaze briefly then looked somewhere past him.

Sophie's arm was looped through his. "Ken—Kade, this is your father, Dale."

Hello, Dad? G'day, mate? Kade didn't voice either greeting because neither felt right.

"It's a pleasure to meet you, Mr. Barrington," Annie said, holding out her hand to him.

He shook it. "Dale, please. No need for formality. You must be Annie." He raised his eyes to Kade again. "Sophie told me you and Kade have been friends for a very long time."

"Long enough for me to have an arsenal of embarrassing photos of him"—Annie winked at Dale—"that I'm willing to share."

Dale's smile appeared strained. "I'd like to see any photos either of you have. We have a lot to catch up on. So much time was lost." His face paled. "So much."

Hugging his arm, Sophie said, "We've found him, Dale. That's all that matters."

Grant and his fiancée's arrival was a welcome reprieve from the silence that followed Sophie's declaration. He shook Kade's hand.

Viviana smiled at Annie. "Hi. I'm Viviana." She hugged her then stepped back and rubbed a hand over her protruding stomach. "I hug for two."

"Annie," Annie said. "How far along are you?"

"Not far enough, despite how it looks." She tipped her head to grin at Grant. "That's why having a wedding here is ideal. We'll get it over with while we're here then head home while it's still safe for me to fly."

Grant put an arm around her waist. "Get it over with, huh?"

She chuckled. "You know what I mean." She looked to Kade and her expression changed. "As long as that's okay with you. When I suggested it, I wasn't thinking about how difficult this might be for you. If it's too much, just say so.

Really, it's not going to be anything fancy. No bridesmaids or groomsmen. Just a ceremony and food. A lot like today, but I'll be in a wedding dress if I can find a tent-sized one." When Kade didn't immediately respond, Viviana added, "I'll cancel it. It's too much—"

"No, it's good," Kade said abruptly. He'd meant to say it with more conviction. He didn't want to be the reason Grant and Viviana weren't married before they had their baby, and he was actually beginning to like the couple. Grant didn't say much, but when he did it was calm and respectful. Viviana was a bubbling fountain of genuine excitement and smiles. They were a good fit for each other. "Your family is already here. It makes sense to do it now."

That's all it took for Viviana to wave her father over to introduce him. Kade shook his beefy hand and nodded. He could see where Connor and Dylan got their height from. Thankfully, he didn't share their personalities.

"I'd introduce you to my sons, but they wandered off," the man said.

"We met them on the way in," Annie supplied. "They're headed to town to my father's pub for the free beer I offered them."

"Sounds about right," the older man said with a smile. "They're good boys, but they can get a little wild."

Grant looked as if that were something he liked about them. "Annie, if you give us the address, Viv and I will collect them later. We'll give them a chance to enjoy themselves a little first."

Annie gave Grant the address and directions on how best

to get there.

Viviana waved toward a table of food that was set up on the other side of the pool. "Annie, I don't know if you're hungry, but I'm starving. Would you like to make a plate up with me? You know, so I won't look like the only one who can't wait?"

Annie glanced at Kade with uncertainty. He nodded once to reassure her. Despite what Dax had said, everything was going relatively smoothly.

"I am rather hungry," Annie said, stepping away to join Viviana.

Grant addressed Viviana's father. "I could eat. What about you? Hungry?"

"Always." He shook Kade's hand one last time. "Great to meet you, Kade."

"You, too," Kade said sincerely. Maybe Annie was right, and he could look at these people as simply *more* of his family.

"So, you met Connor and Dylan?" Dale asked.

"I did." Kade wasn't used to not knowing how to talk to someone. In his line of work, he met all types of people. Heading into the bush with them had a way of bonding people. Many came back year after year, becoming friends as well as clients.

But Sophie and Dale? They had an expectation of a relationship Kade didn't know if he was capable of.

Sophie chuckled. "Look at his knuckles, Dale. He has some Asher in him."

Dale didn't laugh . . . didn't even smile. "Asher is one of

your brothers."

"I know," Kade said. "I read about your family last night."

"Your family too," Dale said thickly then stopped and swayed on his feet. "I'm sorry. I need to sit down for a minute."

"Are you okay?" Kade asked, taking him by the arm, prepared to physically assist Dale as he would any person who looked unsteady on their feet.

Sophie's eyes widened. "Did you take your medication, Dale? You know what the doctor said. If you feel any pain you have to take it right away."

"I'm not in pain, at least not more than I deserve." Dale pulled away from Kade. "I'm fine. I just need to sit down." He turned and started to walk way.

His departure stung of rejection, and that thought must have shown on Kade's face because Sophie looked torn. She touched Kade's arm. "He feels so guilty. I wish I knew how to ease his pain."

"It'll be okay, Sophie." Kade put his hand over hers and hoped he was right. The truth was he didn't know these people or if anything would ever be okay again.

"Dale was always the one taking care of me. I have to go to him, Kade," Sophie said and gave his arm a squeeze. She hesitated and searched his face.

He could feel her plea, so he said, "I'm fine."

"I'll be right back," Sophie said then rushed after Dale.

Before Kade had a chance to digest that conversation, three of his brothers encircled him with their wives and children in tow. Introductions were made with mind-spinning speed. Asher introduced his wife, Emily, and Joseph, their young son who babbled and waved a spit-covered hand at him. Asher looked like a man who had a high opinion of himself. *So this is the one I'm supposed to be so much like?* To Kade the similarities didn't go beyond hair and eye color.

Lance introduced his wife, Willa, along with the twin baby girls they held—Wendy and Laney. He looked exhausted, but happy. Everything about Lance supported what Kade had heard about him. The nice brother.

Ian stood by himself, watchful in a way that reminded Kade of when Dax had said that not all of his brothers would react the same way to his entry to their lives. Although Ian paired a smile with an offer to shake Kade's hand, there was no warmth in his eyes.

An uncomfortable silence followed the introductions. Willa took Laney from Lance and asked Emily if she wanted to take the children into the shade. Emily looked reluctant to leave Asher, but her husband lowered their little one to the ground, and she led him away with Willa.

Lance was the first to speak. "So, this probably couldn't be more awkward, could it?" He clapped Kade on the back. "The good news is you look so much like us that a blood test isn't necessary."

Kade studied the expressions of his two less enthusiastic brothers. "If there is any doubt I'm open to having one done."

"I'm sure it's not necessary," Lance rushed to assure him.

"I'll make the arrangements," Ian added smoothly. According to his online bio, Ian worked for the government in international relations. Kade had come across all walks of life given the job he had, but it was rare to meet someone with such a big-city coldness to him. Ian Barrington wasn't the sort of man he'd eagerly share a beer with at the end of a long day. Which was fine because he didn't see any of these people spending much time in Bright.

Asher folded his arms across his chest. "It's difficult to believe you had no idea Pamela and Dave weren't really your parents."

Kade mirrored his stance. "They *are* in every way that matters."

Asher's eyes narrowed. "Relax. You're too old for a custody battle. I'm just curious how much of your story is true and how much has been creatively amended."

"Why the hell would I lie?" Kade challenged.

Lance interjected, "I think what Asher is trying to say is we're all interested in your life here."

Bullshit.

Sounding every bit the government official he was, Ian said, "We need the truth—the whole truth. Right now, the media only knows what we've told them: we're reuniting with estranged branches of our family. If you have skeletons in your closet, Kade, no matter what they are, tell us now so we can control how that information is disseminated—if it ever is."

"In other words," Asher said, "keep your mouth shut if the media calls. Don't talk to anyone about any of this.

We've got it under control."

"I don't need you to handle the press for me," Kade said. "I'm perfectly capable of—"

"This isn't about you," Asher ground out. "You say something stupid and the whole family takes a hit."

"We're used to being in the public eye," Ian added. "The less you say the better."

"Is this really what we want our first conversation with Kade to be about?" Lance asked, shaking his head.

"Lance, you think life went to shit when he disappeared? His return has the potential of being a real circus." Asher was unapologetically a dick.

Ian nodded. "Before anything goes further, it's important to clarify everyone's role."

"Role?" *What the fuck?*

Lance gave Kade a sympathetic look then glared at Asher. "Our family did change when Kade was taken. Some of us took it harder than others, but it's time for all of us to heal and move on."

"Move on?" Asher growled. "The press will run with this story if they have a chance to. I don't want our family tragedy to be fodder for a fucking movie nor does anyone else here. Kade needs to keep his mouth shut."

Despite how obnoxiously it had been said, Asher had a point. Kade said, "I have no desire to talk to anyone. After you leave, I want things to go back to normal."

Ian and Asher exchanged a look. A hint of sympathy entered Ian's expression as he said, "Your life is about to change, Kade."

Grant joined the group and the conversation. "But we'll help you make the transition."

"No transition. I'm here to meet all of you. Nothing more than that." If they thought he was after their money, he needed to set them straight upfront.

Another man stepped into the conversation as if he belonged there, even though Kade didn't recognize him. He was impeccably dressed in a suit Kade guessed had cost him what most people made in a year and a smile that said he didn't give a shit about what anyone thought of that. "I'm sorry, I can't miss any of this. Go on."

Asher turned to the man and snapped, "Clay, this is none of your fucking business."

Clay offered his hand to Kade, completely ignoring Asher. "Clay Landon. Don't listen to Asher. I never do. There's no going back, Kade. You're rich now. Not as wealthy as I am, but if you work with Grant, all your financial woes will be a thing of the past."

Kade didn't move. Only once Clay shrugged and dropped his hand, did Kade say, "I don't have financial problems. I own my own business. I live a comfortable life. My parents will be well cared for. I don't need anyone's money."

Grant intervened in his calm voice. "It's your money, Kade. Your inheritance."

Asher shook his head as if disgusted. "You hit the lottery. Why bother to pretend you'd rather be escorting old people into the mountains and kissing their asses for tips when you'll no longer have to?"

That's it. Kade dropped his hands and fisted them at his sides. "I like my life here. I'm not looking to change it. And I don't give a rat's ass what you think about what I do. In my best scenario of how this works out: getting to know you is over after this conversation, you guys go home, we send Christmas cards, and that's it."

Asher's response was a sarcastic laugh.

Kenzi's voice broke in, "What's going on?"

Shaking his head, Asher said, "How fucking sad is this? The one who was stolen is the only one of us with a life he doesn't want to change."

Kenzi put her hand on Asher's arm. "Asher. Stop."

Kade leaned in, going nose to nose with Asher. "What is your problem?"

Asher met him with equal aggression. "While you were blissfully living here with kangaroos, our family was dealing with your death, or what we were told was your death. Our mother has been through enough, and you're only adding to it."

"How am I doing that?" Kade growled.

Asher growled right back. "By making this about you and what you want. I don't give a shit what you want. She's been through hell and back because of you. Fucking fake happy."

Another brother, Andrew, joined the group and moved to stand beside Kade, facing off against Asher at his side. "Back off, Asher. You're being an ass."

Asher met Andrew's gaze, frowned, but didn't back down. "He needs to know the score. You, of all people, should understand we need to protect the ones we love."

Angry color filled Andrew's cheeks, but his eyes never wavered. "Don't do it, Asher. Don't fuck with me or Helene. You won't like the outcome."

Kenzi inserted herself between Andrew and Asher. "Everyone take a deep breath. This is not easy for anyone." She looked from Andrew to Asher and back. "I know that beneath all this male posturing, you actually love each other, but Kade doesn't. How do you think this looks to him? Would you want to be part of this family if this was your first impression of us?"

Asher sighed audibly. "You know I'm right." He looked at Andrew. "However, what you decide to share or not is none of my business."

Grant put a hand on Asher's shoulder. "Everything has a time and a place. It doesn't all have to be discussed today."

Asher shrugged his hand off. "I prefer to rip the Band-Aid off."

Ian rolled his eyes skyward. "We know, Asher. But there's a place for diplomacy, even here."

Kenzi shook her head. "No, there's only room for love and forgiveness. I know you're confused, Asher, but if your son disappeared and we found him, how would you want us to welcome him home?"

Asher's eyes sought his wife and child across the patio, and his shoulders slumped. He rubbed his hands over his face. "Fuck." It was an interesting exchange to watch. Asher brushed off reasonable arguments. Threats escalated his anger. One mention however of his wife and child and he backed right down.

Clay said, "Kade, for Asher that's practically an apology."

"Why are you still here?" Asher asked Clay.

Clay smiled and shrugged. "I married into the family, remember?"

Dax appeared beside his friend. "Clay, knock it off."

Ian moved to stand next to Asher. "There were things that needed to be said, and they have been. Kade understands now how much we all have to lose. I'm sure he also sees how things will go better if he works with us rather than against us."

Kade looked around at his supposed gene pool. "Maybe we *should* start with a blood test."

Asher smiled. "Funny."

"Not joking," Kade countered.

Grant nodded to Asher and Ian. "Let's get a drink." When no one moved, he said, "It'll give everyone time to bask in how well today is going so far."

After the three of them were out of earshot, Kenzi turned to Kade. "Asher comes off strong, but he means well. He's just worried about our parents and doesn't know how to handle that."

Dax gave Kade an *I told you so* look.

Kenzi caught the action and elbowed Dax then turned to Kade. "You have to understand, as the eldest, Asher remembers our family before you were taken. I don't. He, Grant, and Ian knew a happier version of our family and losing you changed all that." She looked over at Lance and Andrew. "We were each affected by your disappearance, and we're all working through how it feels to have you back. Give us time to figure it out." Her gaze returned to Kade. "I promise you, we're worth it."

"They are. That's why I'm here." Clay joked, "Kade, your family is as crazy as they come, but they marry the nicest people. They should have led off with the women."

Kade sought out Annie in the mix. She was holding a baby, laughing at something one of the women said, and looking perfectly at ease.

Hell, I might actually have something in common with my brothers. Annie's a hundred times better person than I am.

He frowned. Not that she's mine.

It might have been because his emotions were running high, but he couldn't pull his gaze from her. What would happen when the Barringtons went home? Would he and Annie naturally drift back to their separate lives? His gut clenched at the idea.

No, this time will be different.

"Looks like your girlfriend agrees with me," Clay joked.

"She's not—" He almost said she wasn't his girlfriend, but denying her that title didn't feel right. There was no one else he could imagine at his side for something as monumental as this. In one way or another, he'd loved Annie his whole life. What that meant now he didn't know. "It's complicated."

Dax nodded and put an arm around Kenzi. "It always is."

"I thought you might need this," Lance said, returning with two glasses of beer. "Quite a day, huh?"

"You can say that again." After accepting the drink, Kade downed half of it in one gulp. Annie must have felt Kade's gaze on her because she turned, smiled, and waved. Kade's heart began to thud wildly in his chest.

After a general silence fell over the group again, Kenzi said, "Kade, you and Andrew share a lot of similar interests. He loves the outdoors. In fact, he and Helene run a large animal rescue in Florida."

It was a stretch, but Kade appreciated that Kenzi was trying to build connections between them. He decided to as well. "I read that you had served in the Marines. I'm sure you have jumped out of your fair share of planes."

"I have," Andrew said without emotion.

"While you're here, if you want to try paragliding, I could take you to a great spot."

Andrew took a step back, looking like he'd rather be anywhere but there, "Sorry, Kade. I'm not the brother you should bond with." Without saying more, he turned and walked away, joining his wife and her parents.

Kenzi touched Kade's arm. "He doesn't mean that, Kade. He needs time too. Why don't you tell us about your business. You used to run it with your—with Dave—your adoptive father?"

Kade looked across at Annie again. She was still smiling and enjoying herself. He watched her introduce herself to his brothers as they joined that group. It seemed like a much less eventful encounter than what he'd just experienced, and it inspired him to keep trying.

He turned back to Kenzi and began to tell her about his

life in Australia. Even though he was counting the minutes until he could leave, he didn't rush. Sophie joined them, asking questions about his life in general and his childhood. She seemed genuinely happy to hear that it had all been good.

He asked them about Massachusetts and was surprised at how down-to-earth they both sounded. Kenzi said she traveled with Dax when his work took him away and spent time with family or friends when she wasn't involved in a community project. Sophie said she was cutting back on planning events now that she had grandchildren. She said she loved having babies and chaos in her home again.

"I can imagine Mum saying the same thing. She misses my soccer mates and me hanging at the house after matches. They ate everything in the fridge and made the house smell like a locker room, but she always says she'd trade quiet and clean for a few more of those days." As soon as he said it he wished he hadn't. Sophie's eyes filled with tears. He wasn't sure if it was because he had called Pamela his mother or because she wished she'd had those experiences with him herself. ,

Sophie took one of his hands in both of hers. "You love your life here, don't you?"

He needed to be honest. "I do. I have two really good parents who gave me a great childhood."

She sniffed and blinked a few times then smiled. "When you're ready, I'd like to meet them. I meant what I said about being grateful to them for how good they were to you."

Annie's arrival saved Kade from having to respond. He released Sophie's hand. "Still good?" he asked Annie. After the emotional roller coaster he'd just been on, he was exhausted.

"Great. Everyone has been so welcoming." She searched his eyes. "You?"

Only because their conversation was not private, Kade answered, "I'm glad I came."

She continued to study his expression then asked, "I don't know about you, but I'd love to play a game of volleyball. I saw a net on the other side of the pool." She glanced at Kenzi. "Do you play?"

Kenzi clapped her hands in excitement. "I haven't in years, but I'd love to." She looked up at her husband who was dressed in a charcoal suit. "What do you think? You up for it, old man?"

"Anywhere, anytime," Dax said as he slid off his jacket and began to roll up the sleeves of his dress shirt.

Smiling, Kenzi asked, "Do you think Clay would?"

"If we tell him he can't, yes," Dax said dryly.

Kade chuckled. So far, Dax was his favorite Barrington, even though technically he wasn't one. *Volleyball dressed up like everyone is about to head off for an office job—this should be interesting.*

Suddenly uncertain, Kenzi turned to Kade. "Do you mind if I ask everyone to join in?"

Kade looked across to where his brothers were gathered. He could refuse. In fact, the day would be a whole lot simpler if he claimed he had somewhere he needed to be and left. Based on his first impression of some of them, leaving made sense.

Annie was still watching him closely. He'd never seen her refuse a challenge simply because it might be difficult, and she wasn't doing it now. She could have asked to leave. He wouldn't have judged her for it. That had never been Annie, though, and he doubted it ever would be.

Kade had dated a fair share of women in his life—even thought he'd loved a few of them—but he'd never imagined forever with any of them. His mother and father laughed, fought, made up—and through it all remained supportive of each other. Even after thirty years together, his father still smiled every time his mother walked into the room. They made love look easy. If Kade ever settled down, he wanted it to be with someone who would be a real partner and a best friend as well as a lover.

Someone like Annie.

His traitorous libido unexpectedly threw a variety of provocative images at him. Annie smiling at him while dropping her shirt to the floor. Annie naked on a blanket by the stream where they used to fish together, beckoning him to join her.

What the hell am I doing?

"Kade?" Annie's voice jarred him back to reality. "Are you okay?"

Kade ran a hand through his hair. Now that he'd imagined being with Annie, it was hard to shake his desire. "Yes. Sure. Let's play volleyball."

"I'll go get everyone," Kenzi said.

"Sounds good." Spiking a few balls at his brothers' heads would be bloody satisfying too. That brought a smile to his face.

Chapter Eight

ARLY THAT EVENING, Annie fastened her seat belt then waved at the Barringtons gathered on the front veranda. Although she and Kade had started leaving nearly thirty minutes earlier, disengaging had proven more difficult than even Annie had imagined. Sophie had hugged her—two, maybe three times—in farewell. Kenzi had done the same.

It was beautiful and exhausting.

Kade also waved as he pulled away, looking relieved to go. He didn't say anything for a long time, seeming to need time to process the day—who wouldn't?

Only when he pulled up in front of her apartment did he finally speak. "I can officially tag that the longest day of my life."

"Do you want to talk about it?"

He flexed his hands on the steering wheel. "With anyone else I'd say no. I'm done. I have nothing left."

"I came to support you. Don't feel that you owe me a rehash, Kade."

He unclipped his seat belt and turned toward her, his eyes burning with emotion and something more. "That's the thing, I want to talk it out with you. You're the only part of all of this that makes any sense."

Annie took a fortifying breath, released her seat belt, and turned in her own seat. *This is why I came. This is what he'd do for me. Simple as that.* "Then I'm here for as long as you need me."

His expression darkened. And he rubbed his hands roughly over his face. "I'm sorry I let so much time go by without calling or texting."

Without admitting it had been deliberate, she said, "I'm sorry I didn't make an effort to see you when you came home."

"I thought about you often, Annie."

Oh, God. This is hard. "I thought about you too."

He sighed. "The Barringtons asked to see me tomorrow."

Annie noted he still used their last name as if trying to maintain a distance from them. "I'm sure they want to see you as much of you as possible while they're here."

"I said no."

"Oh."

"I said I had commitments. I don't. I cleared my schedule for the week in case my parents needed me."

Annie held his gaze.

He frowned. "You think I should go."

She lifted and dropped one shoulder.

"I've always known what to do, Annie. Always. Things were clear. Right or wrong. I could trust my gut to tell me the best path. I'm stumbling blind right now. What am I supposed to feel? Because all I am is angry. I don't want this.

God, I sound like a child. It doesn't really matter what I want or don't want. The life I thought I had is gone."

"Of course you're angry." She felt his pain as if it were her own. She took one of his hands between her and held it on her knee. "You had your feet knocked out from under you. I know you, though. You'll find your footing, and this will all work out."

"I hope you're right." He made a disgusted sound. "Did you see my biological father's reaction to me? He couldn't get away from me fast enough. Why bother to meet me at all?"

Running a hand up his arm, Annie felt his tension. "I don't think it's you Dale was running from."

Kade's shook his head, but something in his eyes told her he needed to hear what she'd learned. Annie plowed forward, hoping she was right. "Your sisters-in-law were pretty upfront about the family dynamics and how your disappearance affected your family. Dale lost a son then almost lost his wife to a breakdown. He didn't believe Sophie when she said she'd held you. The doctors told him she'd imagined you alive, so imagine his guilt as he watched her fall apart for years because she had a memory everyone told her was false. He blames himself for how long it took to find you. He's torturing himself with the possibility that had he believed her, it might have not only saved her that pain, but might even have led to finding you. That's a heavy guilt to carry. No wonder he can barely look at you."

"Then not seeing him tomorrow is an act of kindness."

I don't agree, but who am I to tell him what to do in a situ-

ation so far beyond what I've ever experienced? Really, isn't the best decision whatever he feels comfortable with?

Kade laced his fingers through hers, and his gaze remained on their hands as he spoke. "You don't agree."

"What I think doesn't matter." She turned her attention to something outside the window of the car.

He cupped her chin and turned her face so she was forced to meet his eyes. "It matters more than you know."

Don't. Defiantly, her heart began to beat crazily. Her breath caught in her throat as she basked in the full attention of the only man who had ever been able to set her on fire with just a look. His eyes burned with an answering hunger—or was it her imagination? How many more times did he need to leave her before she conceded he'd never feel for her the way she felt for him?

She pulled her face free and shifted farther back from him. "Then I think you need to spend time with your family tomorrow. I know today was hard for you, and maybe they didn't all say or do everything right, but they've been suffering a long time. They didn't abandon you—you were stolen from them. They deserve a second chance—a third if they require it. You've always been a good son, a good friend. The Barringtons need that from you right now."

"I don't know that I can be that for them." He sat back in the driver's seat, expelled a harsh breath, and stared at the roof of the Ranger. "I was in a good place. I knew who I was and what was important. I don't want to be *rescued* from my life here. There is no Kent. They want to spend time with someone who doesn't exist."

His reluctance to see them again made sense to her. She could have wept then, her sympathy for all involved was that intense. She didn't, though. He needed more from her. "That's not true. They want to spend time with *you*. You are Kade Thompson. Nothing will change that. But you're also Kent Barrington. You're the little baby they mourned. You're their second chance. No, you didn't choose this, but life doesn't always unfold the way we want it to. Don't be such a pussy. Pick yourself up and make the best of it."

His eyebrows rose and fell and he laughed. "There's the Annie I love. You say it as it is."

Not always. "I try." She rolled her hand through the air as if taking a bow. Their eyes met and Annie's heart began to beat double time again. She scrambled to lighten the mood. "There must have been something you liked about today."

He nodded slowly. "Sophie is a sweet woman. Kenzi and Dax are people I can imagine in my life. Lance and Willa were cool. We kicked Asher's and Ian's asses on the volleyball court, and that felt pretty good." He bent closer to her. "By far, though, having you there with me was the best part of the day."

Annie's face flamed and she feared everything she felt was on display for him. She couldn't stop her eyes from half closing in anticipation of a kiss. Her body was humming for his. She could slip out of the car and end this now, but she didn't have the strength to. His gratitude was—confusing.

He leaned in closer and closer until his lips hovered just above hers. The desire in his eyes was unmistakable and one word ricocheted through Annie. *Yes. Yes. Hell, yes.*

"You're important to me, Annie."

Breathe. Now is not the time to pass out. "You're important to me too, Kade."

"I don't want to fuck our friendship up."

"I don't want to either."

"I should leave now."

"Yes," she said in a husky voice.

"I don't want to leave." He ran a hand through her hair.

She shivered with pleasure. She closed her eyes and admitted, "Then stay."

His hand tightened in her hair, but the kiss she expected didn't come. She slowly opened her eyes. He wanted her, but there was something else in his expression. "I can't. Annie, I don't know how I feel about anything right now and . . . I don't want to hurt you."

Disappointment and embarrassment flipped the desire she'd felt to anger. She whipped the door open and sprinted up the steps, down the hallway to her door. Only when she reached it did she realize she'd left her handbag in his car. She slapped her hands on the door and cursed. Rather than a strong, independent woman, she felt like a pathetic fool. Only Kade had ever been able to reduce her to this.

He was behind her an instant later. "I'm sorry, Annie." He slammed his hand on the door beside hers. "Fuck. You were so good to me today, and I repay you by being a complete dick."

Without turning from the door, Annie said, "Please give me my handbag and go home. I'm fine."

"No, you're not. I know you, Annie. I'm not leaving until I know you're okay."

Composing herself, she turned and realized her mistake when the move brought her face to face with him, as close as they'd been in the car. The concern in his eyes made her want to hug him, but also kick him. *Be an ass, so I can finally get you out of my heart.* "Go home, Kade. Today was a long day for both of us." She held out her hand for her purse.

He handed it to her. She dug for her keys then struggled to unlock her door with a hand that was shaking from emotion. He closed his hand over hers, and she froze. When he spoke, it was from right behind her ear. "Annie, I didn't mean to upset you. I wasn't thinking. Today at the lodge, I saw you in a different light, and it confused me. I want to be with you, Annie. Tonight—all night—tomorrow. I don't want to lose you again. I'm trying to be honest. My head is all messed up right now. I don't know what the fuck I'm doing." The heat from his body warmed hers. She closed her eyes and strove for control. His voice tightened with emotion. "I'll leave, but tell me you're okay. Say you don't hate me."

"I could never hate you," Annie said in a strangled voice. She sought the words to tell him how she felt, but when none came to her, she turned and kissed him. She kissed him with all the passion and love she'd fought to deny over the years. She kissed him deeply, wantonly, with every inch of her and every formerly safeguarded corner of her soul.

Kade pulled her full against him and kissed her back hungrily. Any doubt she'd had faded away in the face of their passion. Her body came alive for him in a way it hadn't for those before him. No man had ever lived up to him simply because they hadn't been him.

A little voice tried to warn her to hold back, to protect herself, but she ignored it. He couldn't have been clearer about how he felt. Her body didn't care. This was *Kade*.

She'd explain it to her heart later.

The door opened and slammed shut behind her and they stumbled into her apartment, continuing to kiss as they made their way across the living room. He whipped her shirt up and over her head, tossing it to the floor. She pulled his shirt free of his jeans and tried to do the same. He finished the job for her.

Her bra—she wasn't sure who removed it. Clothing flew from both of them in frenzied abandon until they were blissfully naked skin to naked skin. Kade was strong, hard, and as rough as the high country he loved.

His mouth was hot and confident as it explored her. His hands were bold and commanding. He lifted her and laid her across her bed, looking at her the way she'd always dreamed he would. Spread out before him, she might have felt vulnerable with another man but she trusted Kade. There was no embarrassment, no worry that he wouldn't take care of her. Primal lust, as simple and as beautiful as time, held her spellbound.

As he kissed her breasts, adoring each with torturous skill, he ran a hand up her bare leg to settle possessively on her sex. She moaned, wanting . . . needing more from him. She reached for his cock, encircling it with her hand while he slid a finger between her folds.

He was hard. He was huge.

His fingers were magic.

She bit her bottom lip as she moved her hand up and down his shaft, imagining him already inside her. The thrust of two of his fingers inside her had her gasping and begging for him not to stop. In and out he pumped his fingers, driving her wilder and wilder for him.

"You're so perfect," he whispered.

She shuddered with pleasure. He pulled away for a moment then returned, spreading her legs wide and kissing his way up her thighs to her sex.

If his fingers had been magic, his tongue was pure sin. Front to back and everywhere between, he claimed her as his. She grasped at his shoulders, so close—so ready to explode.

"So fucking perfect." He raised his head, adjusted their position, and entered her with one powerful, balls-deep thrust that took her over the edge. She cried out his name, wrapped her legs around his waist, and opened herself wider for him even as an orgasm rocked through her.

Any trace of gentleness left him. He pounded into her, and she rose to meet each thrust with equal ferocity. It was a primal mating that consumed both of them until she felt her second climax coming and cried for him to join her.

They collapsed into each other's arms. She closed her eyes, hoping he'd do the same, as she tried to gather her thoughts. She and Kade had just fucked. She was old enough to know that sex came in many flavors. Sometimes it was an expression of love. It could be a comfort or connection. This was a release.

"Annie"—Kade ran a hand gently through her hair—"I know you're not sleeping."

She opened her eyes and searched his expression for a hint of what he was thinking. Where would they go from here? He cared about her—that was never in question. How would sex change their relationship? That was the big unknown.

"What are you thinking?" He traced her jaw with the back of his knuckles. "I wish you were the type to blurt things out. I need to know if I should start off with an apology or a victory dance."

"Victory dance? Really?" The corner of her mouth curled with amusement at that.

He bent and kissed her lips lightly while saying, "Only if you agree that was fucking fantastic."

She smiled into the kisses. "It was okay."

His head snapped back and his eyes widened. "Just okay?" He grinned and rolled so she was pinned beneath him. "Annie Martin, you take that back right now."

She laughed. He sounded exactly as he had back in high school when something she'd joked about hit too close to home. "I had no idea you were so sensitive."

She thought he'd laugh along, but his expression turned serious. "Only when it matters, Annie. And you have always mattered."

"I know." Positioned as they were, she wasn't able to withdraw or look away.

"I should have left when you told me to. I couldn't. And then you kissed me." He rolled back onto his side, holding her to him as he did. "I'll fix this."

"What do you mean . . . fix it?"

"I'll be by your side."

She was momentarily lost. "You mean, like if we just made a baby?"

He went a little pale. "Holy shit, I didn't think of that."

She pushed back a little and sat up. "I'm on birth control and you used a condom. We're fine, Kade."

"Good, but that wasn't what I meant." He sat up beside her, in all his naked glory, talking to her as if they were like this all the time together. "Where do you want to take this, Annie?"

To the altar? No way am I saying that. "I don't understand, Kade."

He ran a hand through his disheveled hair. The move made the powerful muscles of his chest ripple. "How do you feel about me? I mean—Christ, this is hard. I want to make sure you're okay."

Annie gripped the sheet to the front of her. She hadn't felt exposed a moment ago, but she did now. "I'm good."

His gaze slid over her slowly, warming her as it did. Her nipples puckered. Her sex clenched in wet anticipation. His cock surged to full attention. "I have no business being here. I want to fall asleep with you in my arms and wake up to you, but—"

"But?" Annie crossed her arms over her breasts.

"God, I'm a selfish prick. I just want—"

"What?" *Do I want to know? I probably don't. No, I need to know.* "What do you want?"

"Beyond the obvious?" He turned, swung his feet to the floor, and stood. His cock waved high and proud as he paced beside the bed. It would have been a comical sight if Annie wasn't finding it difficult to concentrate as desire began to flame within her again. "I've never slept with anyone I cared so much about. God, that sounds bad." He swore again, paced more, then stopped and frowned at her. "Maybe we should start dating and see where this goes."

"Maybe? Or maybe take a deep breath and slow down." *After all he's been through today, he is vulnerable and confused. He never wanted to date me before, why would he now? How will he feel tomorrow or next week? I can't be hurt again.*

"If that's what you want." He sat on the edge of the bed, facing her with real torment in his eyes. "I need to know this won't change things between us. I don't want to lose you again."

Annie blinked back tears and forced a smile. "You won't." She could have declared her love for him then, but Kade wasn't himself. He'd admitted he didn't know how he felt. When he surfaced from this, most likely they would be right back where they'd been—friends. Telling him how she felt about him, how she'd always felt about him, wouldn't have been fair to either of them—not yet. She bit her bottom lip, sucked in a breath, then said, "And stop worrying about me." She took a deep breath and lied. "Sometimes a girl just needs to get laid."

He frowned and looked as if he had a rebuttal to that, but her phone buzzed from her handbag across the room. Kade retrieved it for her, handing it to her with a strange look on his face.

She checked the caller ID. "It's Harrison. I'll call him tomorrow." She tossed her phone on the bed beside her.

Kade crawled onto the bed with a new expression in his eyes. He cupped her chin and ran a thumb over her lips. "Annie, will you have breakfast with me tomorrow morning?"

Desire rocked through her. "Yes."

"And lunch?" He wiggled his eyebrows.

Despite how tempting that was, Annie said, "I have a client I'm supposed to fly to Melbourne tomorrow."

"Dinner then."

"Okay."

He pulled her ever so slowly back into his arms then whipped the sheet from between them. His remorse had been replaced by rock-hard hunger.

Maybe he didn't love her, but he wanted her. She'd spent half her life wishing she could be with Kade. No matter where it led, he was there now, kissing her neck, caressing every inch of her as if she were precious to him. She arched against him, hungrily running her hands over his strong back. If tomorrow took him away from her again, she refused to regret choosing to be with him. She took his mouth with hers, kissed him deeply, and savored every second of it.

AFTER A RESTLESS and brief sleep, Kade woke with Annie's arm flung over his chest and her leg intertwined with his. Her hair was a wild mess—and she had never looked more beautiful to him. He considered waking her, but she was sleeping so peacefully he couldn't bring himself to.

Their conversation the night before came back to him and he cringed. He could hear himself telling her he needed her and remembered too clearly the expression he'd put in her eyes. He'd used her. His love for her as a friend should have stopped him at her door. Although he'd been honest with her, it didn't make what he'd done more palatable.

Annie wasn't a one-night stand woman. She wasn't even the friends-with-benefits type. She deserved to be with someone looking for a relationship.

She wasn't in love with him. They'd only had friend sex. He *should* be relieved.

There was no reason to feel guilty.

Kade slid out from beneath Annie and slowly began to dress. He was confused, but that was nothing new. The last few days had fried him.

It's better if she doesn't love me. I don't know what the hell I feel about anything or anyone right now.

He loved his parents—Pamela and Dave—but no longer with the uncomplicated, blissful certainty of who he'd been a few days earlier. Would the truth change how Dave saw him? Dave had adopted Kade under the misconception that Kade was actually the child of the woman he loved. Now that the Barringtons had descended, would Kade end up with two fathers who couldn't bear the sight of him?

Hell if he knew. His life was no longer neatly following the plan he'd laid out. He was now winging it and hoping it somehow all worked out.

Kade found a piece of paper and pen. He wrote, "Be

back in a few with breakfast," and propped the note on the nightstand next to Annie. She'd rolled over onto her stomach, claiming the entirety of the bed. He fought a strong urge to crawl back beneath the sheets with her. Instead he leaned down and kissed her gently on the forehead.

With a shake of his head, he gathered his wallet and phone and headed to his car. His parents' home was only about two kilometers away, and he made it to his old bedroom without encountering either parent. Intending to be back at Annie's before she woke, he quickly showered, changed, and packed an overnight bag.

He was on his way down the stairs, heading toward the door, when his father said his name. He halted and turned to see both of his parents standing side by side in the living room, with concerned expressions on their faces. "Morning."

"You didn't come home last night," his father said in quiet reprimand.

"Sorry." He finished walking down the stairs and dropped his overnight bag. "I should have called."

His mother stepped toward him. "We're not upset. Just worried about you."

"Are you staying at the lodge?" his father asked, looking from Kade to the bag and back.

"No." Kade had never lied to his father, not even the few times when Kade had gotten in trouble at school. Dave was even-tempered and solid in his support. Discovering that his wife had kept Kade's true identity from him had shaken him, but somehow they were working it out. He felt bad for doubting his father. Dave was the type of man who not only talked about doing the right thing—he lived that way. And he deserved the truth. "With Annie."

"Annie?" his mother asked, her eyes widening with pleased surprise. "I always knew—"

"Is that wise, Kade?" his father cut in.

Kade ran a hand through his hair. "Probably not."

His father shook his head slowly. "Annie has been a good friend to you. Treat her with the respect she deserves."

Kade's stomach twisted in a painful knot. His father wasn't saying anything he hadn't already said to himself. His hands fisted at his sides. One more thing to feel bad about.

Dave looked from Kade to Pamela. "This is a confusing time for all of us, but we'll make it through if we remember to be good to one another."

Pamela's eyes teared up and she slipped beneath his father's arm, hugging him tightly. "Kade knows what he's doing. You taught him how to be a good man."

His parents embraced and a piece of Kade settled. They loved each other. That wasn't a lie either.

Dave returned his attention to Kade. "How did yesterday go with the Barringtons?"

"It was interesting," Kade hedged. "They certainly look like me."

"They seem like very nice people," his mother said. "At least the two we met. Grant and Viviana."

Dave studied his son's face then added, "Relationships don't happen in a day. What feels unnatural now, won't in time."

Kade nodded. His father understood. "Sophie said she'd

like to meet you both . . . to thank you for being so good to me."

"She doesn't hate me?" Pamela asked in a shaky voice. "I was afraid she might—"

"No," Kade answered, hoping to bring his mother some comfort. "She seemed . . . she seems grateful to you. For protecting me."

"And Dale?" Dave asked.

Kade blanched. "He wanted nothing to do with me. Too much for him to deal with, I guess."

"Time, Son. He'll come around." Dave was taking all of this better than Kade had expected.

"I can't say I share your confidence, but that's okay. I don't need him."

"He's your father, Kade."

"No, *you're* my father."

His mother exchanged a look with her husband. "We love you, Kade. In our hearts, you are our son. Nothing will ever change that, but Sophie and Dale are also your parents. Loving them is not a betrayal of us; it's a testament to how we raised you. You're no longer a child I need to protect, and these are not the people I would have ever kept you from. Open your heart to them."

Kade closed the distance between himself and his mother and hugged her to his chest. "I'll try, Mum. All I can promise is I'll try."

His mother hugged him back tightly. "That's all any of us can do."

When she finally released him, Kade picked up his overnight bag again. His father said, "I'll walk you out."

Alone on the front veranda, Kade waited for what he knew his father would say. He deserved it, though, every word.

After a long moment, his father surprised him with a back-thumping hug. "You'll be fine, Kade. Annie will be too. Just remember, everyone makes mistakes. When you don't know what else to be—be kind. Sometimes it's the hardest path to take, but I've never once regretted it."

Kade hugged his father back and blinked a few times quickly as his eyes filled uncharacteristically with tears. "I don't know what that looks like right now."

His father stepped back. "You'll figure it out. Don't you worry." He gestured toward the bag in Kade's hand. "Be careful with her, Kade."

Kade nodded once then headed down the steps to his car. "I'll call you tomorrow."

"Be careful with her . . ." His father's words echoed in Kade's thoughts as he drove to the café near Annie's apartment.

What does careful mean now?

Calling things off?

While he drove, he asked himself some tough questions. Even if she didn't love him, wasn't it unfair to be with her when he was in an emotional tailspin? Was he sabotaging his friendship with her by reconnecting with her while his life was in chaos?

I slept with Annie.

Brave, daring, sweet Annie.

And it was so fucking good.

A SHORT TIME later, he parked his car in front of her apartment with two coffees and a box of pastries teetering on the passenger seat. He didn't immediately get out but sat there wishing he hadn't followed her into her apartment while at the same time marveling he had.

The passenger side door opened. Annie picked up the items on the seat and sat down, closing the door behind her. "Perfect timing," she said with a cautious smile. She was dressed in a summer dress that left her shoulders and neck deliciously bare. Her curls were pulled back in a loose ponytail, reminding him of how she'd looked in high school. So beautiful—so calm. *So Annie.* "Harrison called. Grant went to pick Viviana's brothers up last night, but they were having too much fun to end the night. They thought they could outdrink Harrison. They're passed out on the living room couches at my parents' house. I promised we'd go retrieve them." She secured her seat belt then shot him another smile.

He didn't start the Ranger. "I thought you had to work."

"I called in one of my guys to cover for me. Dad said he was going to deliver those two to the old courthouse lockup if they woke up anything like they came in last night."

"That doesn't sound good."

"Dad can handle them, but I thought you might want company since it looks like you'll be seeing your new family today whether or not you're ready to."

"Annie."

"Yes?"

Everything he'd planned to say flew out of his head. He tucked a loose curl back into her ponytail. "I'm a big boy. Don't feel that you have to put your life aside for this."

Her eyes darkened and she looked away. "You want to see them alone today. That totally makes sense. I shouldn't have assumed—"

He gently turned her face back toward him and cut off her words with a kiss that left them both breathless and shaken. "I want you there, Annie. Holy shit, you're the only reason I survived yesterday. Last night was amazing. I want to be with you tonight. Tomorrow night. But I don't want to screw up our friendship. Have I already done that?"

She covered his mouth gently with her hand. "No more than I have."

He kissed her then, rougher than he meant to. Lust rose hard and fast, making everything else seem instantly insignificant. She met his kiss with equal passion, and everything else ceased to matter. He lost himself in the feel of her against him, the sweet taste of her. Memories from the night before flooded back and deepened his desire for her. His blood rushed downward as he remembered exactly how good she'd felt wrapped around his cock.

He felt like throwing her over his shoulder and fucking her in the backseat or in her bed again. Hell, he didn't care where as long as they didn't stop.

The buzz of Annie's phone prevented him from whipping her shirt up over her head. He broke off their kiss and realized she was still clutching the coffee tray on her lap. The sight of them brought him back to the reality of where they were.

Her phone buzzed again. Delightfully flushed, she fumbled for it in her handbag. After reading a text message, she said, "It's Harrison again. He says Dylan and Conner woke up. Dad wants to test their archery skills. We should hurry."

Chapter Nine

THE RIDE TO the Martin house was short, which was good because Annie was more confused now than when she'd woken up alone. She'd planned how she would act when Kade returned with breakfast. In the mirror, she'd practiced being casual. There was nothing casual about where they'd taken their friendship.

She'd planned to find some sanity during her day away from him.

That plan had fallen to the wayside as soon as Harrison had called about the slumber party two of Kade's family had had at her parents' house. Instantly her concern had been for Kade. He'd said he wasn't ready to see his family again. It hadn't occurred to her that he might not want her by his side when he saw them.

For a moment it'd felt like the same old rodeo ride—the one where she projected how she felt onto him and then got her heart trampled when she was wrong. This time she was determined to keep her eyes open and her heart realistic.

But that kiss.

Lord, that kiss had sure felt like love. It had shaken her

to the core. He'd looked just as moved by it.

No. No. No.

Kade wasn't a liar. He said what he felt. He wasn't in love with her. She needed to focus on that. She was determined to hear him this time. *What does that make us? Friends with benefits? You know, I don't give a shit. Why do people have to label everything? Does trying to stuff things neatly into a little box make anything better? Kade and I are who we are.*

Annie watched Kade's profile while he drove up her parents' driveway. There were dark circles beneath his eyes, and she doubted he'd slept at all that night. It was a reminder that, although what they'd done the night before had shaken her, Kade was dealing with so much more. He parked behind an unfamiliar car. "I wonder who else is here."

"Looks like Grant's rental." His expression tightened.

"Harrison might have called him."

Clenching the steering wheel, Kade frowned without responding.

Annie touched his forearm and his attention returned to her. "Whatever you're feeling is normal, Kade. Talk to me."

His glare wasn't meant for her, she knew that, but it broke her heart to see her normally easygoing friend so tormented. "I don't want the Barringtons here. Your house is the only place I felt . . ."

Had he been about to say *safe*? Perhaps *normal*? She didn't know and it didn't matter. "You're not ready for your two lives to mix."

He nodded, looking relieved she understood. "But I have

to go in there and act as though I am. I like Grant, but I feel . . ."

"Cornered?"

"Yes."

I refuse to be the next one who makes him feel that way. "I'm only basing this on what I saw yesterday, but I bet Grant would understand if you told him that in a nice way."

"Is there a nice way to tell someone to back the fuck up?" he asked with dry humor and ran a hand through his hair.

Annie smiled because he'd asked similar questions when they were younger, and it was reassuring to see the old Kade was still in there. "Kade Thompson, you know there is. Remember when Donovan moved to Bright in fifth grade? He wanted to be your best friend. He scored a locker right next to yours then started walking home with you even though he lived in the other direction. He drove you crazy, but you figured it out."

"I paid Aiden to help him make friends."

Annie's eyes rounded. "Seriously? Aiden never said a word."

"I paid him well." A grin spread across Kade's face. "And threatened him a little." They were quiet for a moment, then Kade added, "My dad said something this morning I hope I can live up to." He cleared his throat. "He said, 'When you don't know what else to be—be kind.' He also said it may not be the easiest path to take, but it's one he has never regretted."

"I love your father," Annie said, bringing both hands to her heart. "He is such a good man."

Kade nodded. "He really is. When I met the Barringtons yesterday, they talked about my inheritance like I'd hit the lottery. Like they were swooping down to save me from misery and poverty. Unlike them, I don't remember ever being afraid or even particularly angry about anything. I got the better deal—even the better father."

Annie bit her lip rather than defend Dale. Kade needed to say these things out loud. He needed to think them out or he'd never get past them. "So, maybe you shouldn't tell Grant to back off. Maybe that's not the kindest path to take. Your biological family came a long way and all they want is to know you, so maybe that means letting them see your life here."

"Annie, do you have any idea how incredible you are?" Kade's expression changed as he looked across at her. For a moment, the rest of the world faded away and there was only the sizzle of their attraction to each other.

"Yes," she joked as she lost herself in his eyes and the wonder of their connection.

He dug a hand into her hair and brought her mouth an inch from his. "I don't think you do." He groaned and brushed his lips across hers. Desire muddled what was already a confusing situation. There they were, making out in front of her parents' house like teenagers. Annie couldn't consider it wrong when it felt so right.

A knock on the window behind her jolted them both. Annie nearly dropped the coffees then scrambled to ensure her clothing was all in place. After taking a deep breath, she lowered her window.

Connor elbowed his brother. "I told you they weren't waiting in the car for us. Now we're creepers. Great first impression."

Red-faced, Dylan said, "Second impression. We met them yesterday, idiot."

"Did you just call me an idiot?" Connor snarled.

His brother waved his hands in the air in mock fear. "What are you going to do? Accidentally shoot an arrow through me like you did Mitch's lawnmower?"

"Shut up. That wasn't my fault. He parked it right next to the target."

"Sure, if by *next to* you mean *in the same yard.*"

Annie hid a smile by looking over her shoulder at Kade. The twinkle in his eyes told her Viviana's brothers amused him too. They were impossible not to like.

Grant and Viviana appeared beside the car. Kade cut the engine, stepped out, then opened Annie's door. She placed the tray on the console and joined him. After a brief hesitation, he took her hand in his.

"We came as soon as we heard they were here," Grant said, greeting Kade with a handshake. "We were already on our way when Connor told us you were coming too."

Annie's fingers naturally interwove through Kade's again in quiet support.

Laying a hand on her rounded stomach, Viviana said urgently, "I feel so bad. I told your father we'll pay for his lawnmower. My brothers—"

"Are welcome anytime," Mitch said as he joined them. "And your money is no good here." He gave Grant a familiar pat on the back. "You come from good stock, Kade. This one is full of surprises. Last night he made a bull's-eye every time. Never seen anything like it." His gaze fell to Kade's and Annie's linked hands and his eyebrows rose.

"That's kind of you, Mitch," Grant said. "I took archery in high school; I suppose the body remembers. And thanks again for letting Connor and Dylan stay over. We tried to take them back to the lodge last night, but they were determined to stay with Harrison. They think they can outdrink anyone."

Annie welcomed the new topic over any question her father might ask about her and Kade. "Sounds like they met their match in Harrison. He thinks it's funny to test the drinking skills of newbies to his circle."

"I was not drunk," Connor protested.

"No, I wasn't drunk, but you were sloshed," Dylan scoffed. "You fell asleep at the bar."

"It's called *jet lag,* dumbass. I might have taken a brief nap, but you're the one who proposed to the first woman who walked into the bar. You're lucky her boyfriend didn't kick your ass."

Dylan clocked himself in the head. "That was her boyfriend? Man, he should have said something. I was only messing around. Now that I think about it, he did look pissed. Eh, maybe I was drunk. Harrison got us good."

Chuckling, Grant put his arm around Viviana's waist. "And so it comes full circle."

Kade cocked an eyebrow at his brother.

Not looking at all self-conscious, Grant shrugged. "Getting to know Viviana and her family has been a journey. They welcomed me in a similar manner."

Dylan chortled. "I almost forgot about that night." He slugged Kade in the arm. "You'll have to come visit us in the US. You should have seen Grant when we gave him our home brew. He kept saying, 'I love you' and hugging all of us."

Grant smiled. "Sadly, that is not an exaggeration."

Connor pocketed his hands and nodded at Viviana. "We got our asses chewed for it, but it was hilarious."

Viviana rolled her eyes and rubbed a hand absently over her stomach. "It's funny now; it wasn't then."

Connor, Dylan, and Grant exchanged an amused look but not one of them corrected her.

The banter succeeded in reducing Kade's tension. He was smiling right along with them. "Did you really shoot Mitch's lawnmower?" he asked Connor.

"He did," Annie's father chimed in. "That was when we wrapped up the lesson. I have neighbors I like."

Her mother called from the door of the house. "Are you coming in or leaving?"

There was a long awkward pause. Grant said, "I know you're busy today, Kade. We can take Connor and Dylan back."

When all eyes turned to Kade, Annie felt renewed sympathy for him. He was being given an out if he still wanted it. After yesterday, she wouldn't blame him for needing a day away from his newfound family while he came to terms with having them in his life.

Kade looked at Annie for a moment then called out to her mother, "Depends on whether you've already served breakfast or not. I'm starving."

Hazel's face lit up. "Then come on in."

Connor turned hopeful eyes toward her. "All of us?"

She laughed. "Of course, but only if you'll help me in the kitchen. I don't mind cooking, but it always goes faster with extra hands."

"I can make a pancake that will instantly put five pounds on anyone's ass," Dylan declared as he sprinted up the steps.

With a laugh, Hazel held the door open for him. "Sounds delicious."

"Your mother is a saint, Annie," Viviana said.

"She is." Annie smiled. "Your brothers are great too, Viviana."

"They mean well," Viviana said with a pained smile. "My mother died when we were young. My father did the best he could, but they're a little rough around the edges."

"Then they'll fit in perfectly." Annie looked around. "Speaking of rough around the edges, where's Harrison?"

Mitch folded his arms across his chest. "Cleanup duty. Not all the alcohol that went into those three stayed in them. Some graced the floor of the downstairs bathroom."

"I'm so sorry—" Viviana started to say again, but Mitch interrupted her.

"No worries. I like your brothers. What they bring in trouble they make up for in laughs. They're good boys. The right woman will whip them into shape one day."

"I've yet to meet a woman who could handle either of

them for long," Viviana said with an indulgent smile.

"Maybe not in the US." Mitch nodded at Annie. "Aussie women seem laid-back, but they're stubborn. This country was founded by strong women who had to fight to survive. They brought civility to a penal colony, so they can handle those two blockheads."

"Blockheads? That's great." Grant laughed. "I call them meatheads."

Viviana waved a finger at him in playful reprimand.

Grant amended, "In my head. I'd never say it out loud."

"You're in trouble now, Grant," Kade said with a smile.

Viviana put her hands on her hips. "He would be if I didn't know that he loves my family."

"I do," Grant agreed. His smile dimmed when he looked at Kade. "They're a lot less complicated than the family I'm used to dealing with."

Kade tensed.

Annie gave his hand a supportive squeeze.

"What is everyone up to today?" Kade asked.

"Not too much. They'd love to see you . . . if you find you have the time," Grant said.

Annie held her breath. She had no idea how Kade would respond to that.

He took a deep breath before answering. "I'd love to." He met Annie's gaze. "Would you want to go to the lodge after breakfast?"

She swallowed hard. "Sure."

Mitch turned away and started up the stairs. "Come on, let's go help Hazel set the table." He paused and addressed

Grant. "Around here we all chip in. Don't be afraid to wash a dish or two."

Without hesitation, Grant said, "Absolutely."

Viviana hugged Grant. "I have to ask him. Mitch, would you and your family come to our wedding next weekend? It's not going to be anything fancy, but we'd love to have you."

Annie's father smiled and nodded. "We'd be honored to."

Kade took another deep breath.

Grant seemed to catch that his brother wasn't comfortable. He looked like he was searching for a way to give Kade an out if he needed one.

Annie was right there with Grant. She knew Kade probably wasn't ready for the families to mingle on that level, but there was no way to address that without making it awkward.

Oblivious to the change in the mood, Viviana asked, "Of course, you'll be there too, right, Annie? I could use your help leading up to the wedding if you have time and we haven't scared you off yet. You probably know all the best places to get things."

"I do," Annie said slowly. She didn't want to overstep, but she also wanted to help. She tried to gauge what Kade wanted from his expression then decided she could back out later if it made him uncomfortable. "I'd love to help you plan. I could also show you around the area."

Kade looked at her in surprise.

She shrugged. Did he think she didn't see how pregnant Viviana was? She wasn't offering to take her for a hike. "I run a helicopter tour company. It would be easy to take them to the local sites."

"All of us?" Viviana asked with excitement.

Crap, I forgot how many of them were here. "Of course. If you choose a day, I'll make it happen."

Kade leaned down to say into her ear, "Annie, you don't have to—"

Just as softly, she said, "I know I don't have to. I want to. If it's okay with you."

"Ready to go in?" Grant asked Viviana in the background. She agreed and walked away with him.

Kade and Annie stood, simply looking into each other's eyes. "I should end this now. I should spend this week with my family, get my head on straight again, then come to you. I shouldn't have an overnight bag in the back of my car. You deserve so much better than I can give you right now."

She glanced at their linked hands then back up at him. "Do you remember when my aunt Sue came to stay with us so my mum could take care of her? I was fourteen, I think. I was so sad that summer. When she died, it felt like my heart was ripped right out of me. I used to go down to the lake and sit for hours. You sat with me that summer. Even when I told you to go away. Even when your other friends tried to drag you somewhere more fun. You said you wanted to make sure I knew I wasn't alone. Well, you need someone this time, and I'm right here. Everything else will sort itself out. You're not alone and you deserve a friend who will stay even if you tell them to leave."

He hugged her to his chest and shuddered against her.

Her eyes filled with tears, but she blinked them back.

"Besides, it's hard to walk away from great sex."

He lifted his head, a slow grin spreading across his face. "Aha, I knew it was great for you too."

She slid a hand behind his neck and pulled his face down to hers. "It's your humility I find irresistible."

He growled against her lips. "If that's what you've named my cock."

"Annie and Kade," her mother called from the doorway. "Breakfast is ready. Wrap it up."

Chapter Ten

"GOOD, YOU'RE HERE."

Kade groaned at the sound of Asher's voice. It had probably been too much to expect the good mood he'd found during breakfast at the Martin's would carry over to lunch with the Barringtons.

His second arrival at the lodge had started off on a better note than his first. Rather than being met by everyone all at once, he and Annie were greeted by the happy couple: Lance and Willa. They were basking in the freedom of having just successfully put their twins down for a nap with Sophie on standby in the next room.

"She'll probably nap too," Lance had joked, "but our little ladies have quite the lungs on them so we're good. No need for a baby monitor when we could hear them from the garden."

Willa blew a loose curl out of her eyes. "No one will ever wonder what they want."

"That's for sure," Lance agreed, before pulling his wife close and kissing her on the forehead. "Do we have to teach them to speak?"

"I'm afraid so," Willa said with a smile.

Yes, that was how the visit had started—comfortable and promising. Annie had fallen naturally into a conversation with Willa and they'd wandered off. Lance had walked with Kade through the foyer of the lodge toward the back where the women had gone.

All that came to a crashing halt with the arrival of Asher. Lance smiled at his scowling brother. "Hey, Asher."

"Lance, I need to speak to Kade." *Alone* wasn't stated, but it was heavily implied.

Lance looked from one to the other, squared his shoulders, and stood in quiet support of Kade. Although Kade had had friends and Harrison, he'd never actually had a brother go into battle for him. It was confusing especially since the battle was against another family member.

Lance's protectiveness moved Kade in a way he hadn't expected. Was this what it would be like to have a brother?

Or was Asher what having a brother really was like?

Asher didn't appear any happier than he had the day before. Kade appreciated Lance's loyalty, but he didn't want him to have to choose sides. He could handle Asher on his own. "Lance, please tell Annie I'll be out there in a few minutes."

"Sure." Lance hesitated, then said, "Asher—"

"I know." Asher raised a hand to signal him to stop.

"I hope you do," Lance said with a shake of his head before he walked away.

The silence that followed was heavy with the tension of their first meeting. Kade held back what he wanted to say.

He swallowed his anger and waited. *"When you don't know what to be, be kind . . ."* His father had always pushed Kade to be the best version of himself. *I'll try, Dad, but they don't make it easy.*

Asher flexed his shoulders then ran a hand through his hair in frustration. "Listen, Kade . . ."

Kade mirrored his stance. He wanted to say, "Just fucking say it," but he didn't. Asher didn't intimidate him at all, and he needed to know that. He'd always believed, though, the weakest man throws the first punch—even when it comes to verbal sparring. *Bring it, Brother. See if it works out any better for you today than it did yesterday.*

Asher sighed, his hands clenching and unclenching at his sides. "About yesterday . . ."

Kade held his gaze and said nothing.

Asher cleared his throat. "I wasn't thinking about how it might feel for you to meet all of us at once. I was worried about my—our parents—and that may have made it seem like I wasn't happy that we found you."

Wait, is he apologizing? It sounded forced and almost scripted. "But you are?"

Still frowning, Asher folded his arms across his chest. "It still doesn't feel real. I keep expecting to hear this is a hoax or a bad dream. Not that—"

"I get it." Finally, common ground. "I feel the same way. One day I knew exactly who I was and things made sense. Suddenly, nothing I grew up believing is true. I'd love to wake up as the old me."

Asher took a moment to digest that, then he lowered his

arms and nodded. "Emily and I had a long talk last night. A *very* long talk. It's important that you know I didn't mean to belittle your tour company. What I should have said was that you'll soon be in a financial place that doesn't require you to work."

"Don't you work?"

"Of course, but I run corporations, Kade. I don't schlep—"

Kade's eyebrows rose along with his temper.

Asher halted and changed course. "Yes, I work."

Kade leaned in. "Let me clear up any confusion you may have. I'm proud of the company my father built. I'm proud of how I expanded it. I don't require your approval or your money to be happy with the life I have here." Neither spoke for long enough that Kade began to wonder if there was anywhere the conversation could go or if he should end it there. *Be kind even if it's not the easiest path.* "But I appreciate that you call me Kade. I'm not Kent. I never was, and I doubt I ever will be."

Asher nodded. "I see that." He flexed his shoulders again. "Sorry about yesterday."

The tension between them began to ebb away. "Did Emily put you up to an apology?"

With a flash of perfect teeth, Asher actually smiled. "She did, but she shouldn't have had to. I handled meeting you poorly. At the end of the day, you're my brother and that matters to me more than it may seem. I want this to work out for everyone involved."

Another thing they had in common. "That's what I want

as well."

They stood there in awkward silence again.

Finally, Asher pocketed his hands and rocked back on his feet. "So, Annie seems nice."

"She is."

"And you've known her for a long time?"

"Practically my whole life."

"Good, but be cautious even with her. Like it or not, Kade, you're about to come into a sizeable fortune. It'll change how people see you, how they treat you. Everyone will want to know you, but often it won't be for the right reasons."

"Annie doesn't care about money."

"Everyone does."

"How sad for Emily that you think that."

Asher's eyes narrowed, then he flashed his teeth again in a semblance of a smile. "Touché. Emily is different. For your sake, I hope Annie is as well."

Grant entered the foyer. "Everything okay in here?"

"Why wouldn't it be?" Asher countered.

"All good." Kade smiled. He was beginning to get Asher's dry humor. He also respected him more after seeing that he could apologize with the same directness that he could attack. He could trust a man like that. Plus, even though Asher came off as a real arsehole, his wife could obviously knock him down a peg or two. It made Asher more likable. Could he laugh at himself as well? Kade delivered a little jab to test him. "Asher was just apologizing about yesterday." Kade gave his chest a pat. "It was touching."

"Interesting." Grant's surprise was genuine.

Asher arched an eyebrow at Kade. "So, that's how it's going to be?"

Kade shrugged and splayed his hands in mock surrender. "You're right, I should show more respect to my older—my much, much older brother. Kicking your arse yesterday at volleyball was bad enough."

"Hmm," Asher said. "Grant, you can stop worrying about him. He fits in just fine."

Looking pleased, Grant motioned toward the library. "While we're all getting along there are a few things we should discuss. My lawyer put together some documents that require your signature, and then we should go over the schedule for when and what funds will be transferred to you."

"Right now?" Kade asked.

"There's no reason to wait. A lot of this is easier to do while we're all together." Grant led the way to a room that was probably used for board games or as a quiet escape for guests who wanted to curl up with a book from one of many shelves that lined the walls from floor to ceiling.

Rather than a folder of papers, Grant retrieved a laptop from the desk and headed to a sitting area. He motioned for Kade to take a seat then handed him the laptop. "This is just the beginning, of course, but it'll get the ball rolling. Upon completion of a blood test, we'll petition the courts in the US to recognize you as Kent Barrington. Because you were born in Aruba it's complicated. The US allows, but doesn't recognize, multiple citizenship. Ian and I have been working with government agencies here and in the US to determine your best legal route. You don't have to decide everything today, but you may want to consider officially blending your names. For example, Kade Kent Thompson Barrington. Another option is Kade Kent Barrington Thompson, but you might encounter more questions and resistance if you move forward with a different last name. I will, of course, walk you through your financial portfolio as I've designed it. If you're amenable to my continued involvement, I'll guide you toward optimizing your investments and navigating the taxes you'll encounter both here and in the US."

Kade sat and clicked through the first of what looked like an endless list of digital documents. His head was spinning. "Investments? Portfolio?"

Asher sat across from him. "You had a trust fund set up for you when you were born that was disseminated to the rest of us when we thought you were deceased. We've all transferred that amount to an account that Grant is managing for now. Knowing Grant, he'll probably have doubled your net worth by the time he hands your inheritance over to you. We tease him, but he's a genius when it comes to investing."

"How much money are we talking about?" Kade asked, once again feeling as if none of this could possibly be true.

"As of this morning"—Grant sat in a chair beside Asher—"one point five billion. We each inherited less than that, but I factored in the interest you would have accrued over the years had the money been left in an account. Everyone chipped in enough to compensate for that variable."

"Holy shit." Kade nearly dropped the laptop. *One point five billion? Bloody hell.* "You're serious."

Asher leaned forward, resting his elbows on his knees. "I told you—it's a sizeable fortune. I'd suggest you get a bodyguard, but Dax already has someone assigned to you. He's like that."

"Assigned to me? Like following me?"

"Following, watching, paid to take a bullet for you—however you want to look at it." Asher said it so nonchalantly that Kade thought he was joking at first, but he wasn't. "You could get your own team, but we have vetted connections."

Was that the privilege money afforded his bio family? The idea was repulsive to him. "I don't want to pay someone to take a bullet for me," Kade said slowly.

"Who the hell does? We do what we have to." Asher shook his head.

"Asher, you make it sound like we walk around with targets on our backs. Yes, we have to be careful, but you're painting an unnecessarily extreme version for him." Grant waved for Asher to stop.

Asher threw both hands in the air as he surged to his feet. "Sorry, wouldn't want my brother who was switched at birth and targeted for murder to think life wasn't all hiking and drinking beer."

Grant rose to his feet as well. His expression was sympathetic rather than confrontational as he faced off against Asher. "None of this was your fault, Asher. We had no reason to believe Kent was still alive."

Asher punched the back of the chair beside him. "Mom knew the truth. If any one of us had believed her—"

"Stop second-guessing what we could or should have done. Patrice is dead. Let your anger die with her. We have our brother back. No one, not even you, Asher, can fix yesterday. But we can welcome him home. We can make this easier for him. Don't be a hammer when that isn't what Kade needs. Be the good brother you've always been to me." Grant put a hand on Asher's shoulder.

Asher's mouth twisted in an ironic half-smile. "Have I been that good of one?"

Grant gave his shoulder a shove. "I'm cutting you some slack."

It was only when Asher turned back to face him, that Kade realized he'd been watching the conversation as if it were a tennis match. He placed the laptop on the cushion beside him and stood. Part of him wanted to tell both of these men he didn't need either of them. He felt sorry for *them*. His disappearance had indeed fractured the Barringtons.

Just as Lance had stepped up and come to Kade's defense earlier, Kade felt suddenly protective of both Asher and Grant. Kade remembered something Asher had said during their first meeting. *"How sad is this? The one who was stolen is the only one of us with a life he doesn't want to change."* Asher was married to a good woman and had a child and was apparently filthy rich. What could he possibly want to change?

They all feel guilty even though they're the ones who have suffered. "Asher—"

"Do what you want, Kade," Asher ground out. "Grant's right. The last thing you need right now is a hammer." Asher spun on his heel and was halfway toward the door before Kade had a chance to speak.

The kindest choice came to him then. He spoke firmly. "Maybe so, but I do need you. Both of you."

Asher halted and turned.

"I don't know how to be a Barrington." Kade continued, "I don't even know how to be a Thompson anymore. I'm overwhelmed from just glancing at those legal documents. If any of this puts my parents—Pamela and Dave—in jeopardy, I'll need to learn how to best protect them." He took a deep breath, then added, "If I could snap my fingers and be Kent for you, I would, but until a few days ago I didn't know you existed. I don't expect to do any of this right, but with your help, maybe I won't do all of it wrong."

Grant and Asher exchanged a look.

Asher cleared his throat. "I'll never be the brother to turn to if you need a hug, but I'll always have your back. If you consider Pamela and Dave your family, then they're our family as well. We won't let anything happen to them."

"Thank you," Kade said in a thick voice.

With a smile, Grant said, "Hug him anyway. I will now that I know he doesn't want me to."

"Don't expect that to work out for you." Asher narrowed his eyes at Grant, but he didn't actually look angry. "Either of you."

Grant shrugged. He elbowed Kade in the side. "The trick

is to do it in front of Emily. He doesn't say boo when she's around."

"Are you sure you want to start this, Grant?" Asher asked.

"What did I miss?" Ian asked smoothly as he entered the room.

Asher arched an eyebrow. "Grant was just saying how you've been too hard on Kade."

Ian shot a doubt-filled look at Asher. "*I've* been too hard on him?"

"Absolutely." Asher smirked, as he gave Ian shit the same way Kade had given him earlier. "I believe he said you need to chill the fuck out."

"That doesn't sound like Grant," Ian said, looking back and forth between his brothers.

"Why would I make it up?" Asher asked with a completely straight face.

"It's true," Grant said, playing right along with Asher. "I said it right before he offered to teach Connor and Dylan how to play chess. They'll be so excited when I tell them."

Asher put his hands on his hips. "You wouldn't dare."

Grant's face lit with a grin. "Oh, I dare."

Ballbusters. Kade liked it. This was a side of his brothers he could relate to. He smirked as he imagined the suit-clad, take-no-bullshit Asher attempting to teach Viviana's brothers anything.

Asher shrugged and said to Kade, "I'd tell him where to go, but he knows more about where my money is invested than I do."

Ian sighed and rolled his eyes. "Here we go."

Grant flexed his shoulders beneath his pristine charcoal suit. "Do you know why your name will never come up on a card during Charades? Because it would be too easy. All I'd have to draw is a sphincter."

Asher threw back his head and laughed. The rest joined in—even Kade. And it felt good.

A movement in the doorway caught Kade's attention. Annie had come back for him. Their eyes met and the wonder of the moment continued as she seemed to understand exactly what was going on. She motioned that she was getting something to eat and for him not to rush.

He nodded and watched the door for a moment after she'd gone.

"Friends? Right," Asher said.

Ian interjected, "Asher, it's none of our business."

"I like her," Grant said. "Our gene pool would benefit from another infusion of normal."

"At least he didn't say average," Asher joked.

Kade scanned the faces of his brothers. "Sorry?"

Asher thumped Kade's back. "Let's just say you shouldn't take relationship advice from Grant."

Grant puffed up in mock offense. "Or real estate advice from Asher."

Ian chuckled. "Both are good stories for another day. Mom and Dad are waiting outside."

As Asher headed toward the door he said, "I'll tell you anything. My life is an open book. Unlike Ian's. Everything is top secret with him. If he wasn't my brother, I doubt I'd have the clearance to talk to him."

"That's definitely a fact. Too many shady deals in your past," Ian retorted with a smile. "Grant would always be welcome, though."

"Bastard," Asher said then laughed.

Kade was on the outside of these jokes, which served as a reminder that he was not one of them—not yet anyway. Grant must have sensed his train of thought, because he moved to walk beside Kade. "So, where do you have your savings currently located?"

"At a bank?" Kade answered what he thought was a ridiculous question and saw a flash of horror come and go on his brother's face.

Grant patted his shoulder. "It's better than burying it in the backyard or under your mattress, I suppose. It's okay. We'll start simple."

Viviana met them in the hallway and slid beneath Grant's arms. "Tell me you're not lecturing Kade on his finances."

Grant didn't deny it, but he did flush. "He said he was open to guidance."

Viviana winked at Kade. "If he calls you average, kick him right in the balls." She rubbed her stomach. "He'll heal up by the time I need him again."

Grant pulled his pregnant wife to him and kissed her on the lips. "It's her sweet nature that drew me to her."

A sudden picture formed in Kade's mind as he looked the couple over. "Grant, did you call your wife average?"

With an amused groan, Grant threw up one hand. "It

was when I first met her and out of context it sounds damning, but I was attempting to explain that the night I'd met her I'd deliberately sought out someone—"

"Grant, I love you, but it's insulting in any context." Laughing, Viviana placed her hand on Grant's chest. She hugged him and turned her attention back to Kade. "My husband means well. We're still working on the way he phrases things."

Kade was about to throw back something Grant had said earlier, but changed his mind before he uttered it. Grant had been nothing but kind to him, and he didn't know if they yet had that kind of relationship.

Grant narrowed his eyes, but he didn't look upset. "Say it. You know you want to."

Kade smiled, still holding it back. "I don't know what you're talking about."

At Viviana's nudging, Grant admitted, "I was complimenting his choice of Annie. I may have said our gene pool would benefit from another infusion of normal."

Hand to forehead, Viviana burst out laughing. "You didn't."

Kade's smile widened. He could get used to these people in his life. "He did."

"What am I going to do with you?" Viviana joked at her husband.

Grant hugged her closer as they started walking again. "Stick with me forever because you love me and someone needs to keep me in check?"

Glowing, Viviana beamed a smile. "Sounds like a solid

plan."

They all exited out to the back veranda where Annie was gathered with the others. She looked up from her conversation with Lance and Willa and waved at Kade as he approached. When he joined the group, he took her hand in his . . . and it felt right.

Were they meant to be more than friends? He was confused. Part of him wanted to slow down with her, wait until his life settled before trying to figure out how he felt for Annie.

Another part of him, the part that had gathered his things from his parents' house, had no intention of separating from her now. Right or wrong, friends or more, she was his port in the storm.

Is that fair to her? Is it how I'll feel when the Barringtons leave and things go back to normal? *But things won't ever go back to the way they were—not my family—not me and Annie.*

"Are you okay?" she whispered. "You look worried about something."

"No, I'm good." He leaned down and kissed her temple gently. "Have I told you how much I appreciate you?"

Her expression fell and she look saddened by what he said. He wished they were alone so he could ask her why, but the moment passed and she smiled, even tugged on his arm so he'd bend closer to her. "Yes, but you can show me later."

A burst of lust brought his introspection to an end. He'd be in her bed that night. She was back in his life and it felt right. That was as much as he knew and as far as he could presently plan.

LATER THAT NIGHT, naked and cuddled against Kade, Annie closed her eyes and basked in the afterglow of their lovemaking. She rested her hand on his chest as it rose and fell in deep even breaths. He held her close even as he slept. Their legs were intimately intertwined. Heaven. There might be a price to pay for it later, but she'd waited her whole life to be where she was.

One question pestered her, marring what otherwise would have been bliss. Would he be there if he knew she was in love with him? Would she lose him if she told him now?

He shifted. Her eyes flew open.

"What's wrong?" he asked, his voice deep from sleep.

She caressed his strong jaw. "Nothing."

He dug a hand in her hair and tipped her head back. "You know you can't lie to me. I know you too well."

She lowered her gaze to his chin. "Not as well as you think. It's been a long time, Kade."

"It has been," he said, adjusting his position so his face was closer to hers. "I had to leave, Annie. For my dad . . . for me."

"No worries." She understood. She always had. "I'm good. I'd tell you if I wasn't." Another lie. That was the problem with not being honest—it didn't leave a person with much choice when it came to lying again.

He kissed her lips tenderly then studied her expression. "Good, because I want you to be happy, Annie. I don't know how I would have survived the past two days without you."

"You would have done fine, but you're welcome." She looked deeply into those intelligent, open eyes of his. He didn't have secrets. She didn't want to have one from him, but the risk was too great. He was struggling to make sense of how his life had changed. He wouldn't always be, though. She'd tell him then.

"Guess what, Annie?" His tone lightened, and he smirked.

"What?" Her heart did a funny flip. There was a light in his eyes she hadn't seen before, and she warned herself not to read too much into it, but she held her breath as she waited for his response.

His smile widened and he rolled so she was on top then under him. The sheets tangled around them. "I'm rich. Filthy rich. Like I don't even know if I want that much money kind of wealthy."

"That's great." Disappointment swept through Annie, and she gave herself a mental kick.

He frowned. "Is it?"

She forced a bright smile. "Of course it is." *I'm such an asshole. All I can see is how this will take you away again. You think I'm a good friend? I'm not. I'm trying to be, but I'm failing.* "I'm sorry. I'm happy for you, just tired. Don't read anything into my expression. Tell me everything."

He turned to check the clock on the nightstand then moved back onto his side and hugged her to him. "Two a.m. Go back to sleep; we can talk in the morning." He nuzzled her neck and his cock tented the sheet as another idea came to him. "Or kiss me and we'll find something better to do than sleep."

Her body warmed and she smiled. "Better than sleep?"

She ran a hand down the flat hardness of his stomach, stopping just before his impressive erection. "I do love sleep."

He sucked in a breath and whispered in her ear, "You also love the feel of my big cock deep in your pussy."

Memories of exactly how good it felt brought a flush to her cheeks and wetness to her sex, but she batted her eyes at him and asked, "Do I?"

He growled. "Need a reminder?" His hands ran over her possessively then slid between her thighs as he kissed her deeply. His tongue slid between her lips while his fingers slipped between her folds. His thumb sought her clit and circled it slowly. Two fingers thrust inside her and pumped in and out with a rhythm that drove her wild. Her hand encircled his hard cock, desperate to take him where she was going.

They rolled back and forth over the bed in hot abandon. She couldn't get enough of his taste, of the feel of his body moving against hers.

She gave herself completely over to him. His mouth was her master. His demanding touch a sweet torture as he brought her near release again and again then paused. Finally, she dug her hands into his back, opened her legs wide for him, and was near begging as he positioned himself above her.

He dipped just his tip into her, then pulled out and ran the thick length of him up and down over her clit. She bucked up against him and whimpered into his mouth as his tongue continued its dance with hers.

He pulled back then plunged deeply into her with a

powerful thrust that sent waves of heat rushing through her. She clenched around him, wrapped her legs around his waist, and welcomed him deeper and deeper. Her hands dug into his hair. He broke off their kiss to adjust her so he could put one of her legs over his shoulder.

There was no tenderness in this taking, but she didn't want any. She wanted him to be as out of control as she was, as much a slave to her as she was to him. And he was. Theirs was a rough mating with a climax that left them both sweaty and shaken.

They lay side by side, simply holding hands for several minutes.

He chuckled. "Holy shit, Annie. I needed that."

That.

Not necessarily her.

Annie clenched the sheet with her free hand and cursed beneath her breath. *Why can't I just enjoy being with him? Why do I have to ruin this? It's good, so good. Why can't that be enough?*

"Annie?"

Annie turned her head to meet his gaze. "Yes?"

"Did I mention that I'm fucking rich?" His flash of a smile revealed he was not a mind reader.

She grabbed a pillow and smacked him in the face with it.

He laughed and tossed it off the bed then rolled onto his side and smiled at her. "I'm serious. And if there's something you need, anything you need, tell me. I'd like to repay you in some way for being there for me this week."

She stiffened. "I don't want your money, Kade."

He tapped her on the nose. "Don't go getting all pissy. I know you'd fuck me for free. I just want to do something nice for you."

She shoved him back and sat up. "I'd be careful how you talk while your balls are within grab-and-twist reach."

His hand instantly went to cover his family jewels. "Never threaten the boys. They're sensitive about shit like that." He shot her a playfully apologetic smile.

She laughed. "The boys?"

"You have a better name for them?" He lifted his hand. Even unexcited he was impressive. "This guy is now sadly Humility. He used to be The Rock. Once he was Hercules. I'm not sold on your naming skills."

Their earlier conversation came back to her, and she shook her head while laughing again. "Oh, my God. The Rock? Really?"

He flexed his shoulders. "I was twenty."

Smiling, she lay down beside him, propping her head up on one hand. He'd never held back with her. She couldn't imagine him like this with other women, but maybe he was. Was that why women had flocked toward him his whole life? Did he make them all feel as special as he made her feel? "How many women have you been with, Kade?"

He blinked but didn't immediately answer. "You weren't my first." He wiggled his eyebrows. "Was I yours?"

She rolled her eyes. "Sure."

He cuddled her closer, but his expression had darkened. "I don't want to imagine . . . let's drop this, okay?"

She nodded. She didn't really want to imagine him with anyone else either.

In the silence that followed, Annie sought a way to lighten the mood. "So, how rich is rich?"

"Over a billion."

Her eyes rounded. "Oh, my God. You're serious?"

"Yep." He tensed against her.

His tone told her everything she needed to know. He found it as overwhelming as she did. "I don't even know what I'd do with that much."

He sighed and rested his chin on the top of her head. "Promise me something, Annie."

"Anything."

"Kick my arse if it starts to change me."

"Absolutely." She hugged him.

If I'm part of your new life.

Chapter Eleven

EARLY THE NEXT morning, Kade tossed his overnight bag in the back of his car. He stood, resting one arm on the open door of his vehicle while watching Annie drive off. She had an early run to Melbourne then one back later in the day. A little breathing room would be good for both of them. They'd quickly gone from long-lost friends to passionate lovers. His head was still spinning.

He fought the urge to call her right then and ask her to meet him as soon as she returned. Two days ago he'd wanted her with him because he hadn't wanted to face his family alone. Now he felt her absence with an intensity that was unsettling.

Where were they headed and had she found it as hard to leave as he'd found it to watch her go?

His phone rang. He took it out, still staring blankly down the street where Annie had gone. "Thompson."

"Kade, it's Kenzi. Could you come by the lodge? Dad had a rough morning. He might be going to the hospital. Ian found a local doctor who is in with him now." Her voice was thick with emotion. "You should be here."

"On my way." Kade climbed into his car and slammed the door. Because he'd assured Kenzi he'd be there shortly, he floored it. He almost called Annie, but he didn't know what he'd be walking into, and he'd already laid more than enough family issues at her feet. He did call his parents. Sadly, through experience, his father knew which medical facilities were the best if it came to that. He told them what little he knew and promised to call as soon as he knew more.

He took a corner with screeching tires and cursed when a police siren wailed behind him. He pulled over, retrieved his paperwork from his glove box, and lowered his window.

The tall and lanky officer who leaned down to address Kade thankfully had a familiar face. Officer Shane had graduated from the same high school, and they'd played soccer on the same team for a couple years. "Well, if it isn't Kade Thompson. Heard you were back in town."

"G'day, Shane. Good to see you."

"Same. It's been too long. Where you off to in such a rush?"

Kade shook his head as he tried to compose himself. "The lodge at Lavender Farm. I got news that my—that someone I know is—I don't even know what the hell is wrong with him. I should have asked. All I know is he can't die now when I've just met him. I need time to figure out who he is—who I am—what we're supposed to be to each other." Kade blinked back tears. He couldn't remember crying . . . ever. He wasn't this person. This was not his life.

Shane removed his hat, tucked it beneath his arm. "You drunk?"

Kade rubbed a hand over his eyes. "I wish." He lowered his hand. "It's been a long week."

"Why don't you step out of the car, Kade, just so I know you're safe."

Kade opened the door . . . grudgingly. "See, sadly sober."

Shane looked him over, then nodded. "Who's at the lodge?" Kade's fatigue was definitely catching up with him as he blinked to avoid the bright morning sun reflecting from Shane's badge with blinding intensity. "Dale Barrington, my biological father." Bright was a small town. He'd know soon enough.

"I didn't know you were adopted." Shane looped a thumb into his duty belt at his waist.

"I didn't either."

"And he's sick?"

Kade shrugged. "When I got the call a doctor was determining how serious it is. I should be there."

The blessing of having grown up with almost everyone in Bright was that Shane not only believed him but cared. He used a radio on his uniform to call in that due to a possible medical emergency he'd be escorting a car to the lodge.

"Thanks, Shane." Kade held out his hand.

Shane gave it a firm shake. "Good to have you back, Kade. Don't be a stranger. Mum would love to see you." It was then Kade remembered Shane had lost his father to illness at a young age.

"I'll drop by soon," Kade promised, returning to the driver's seat of his car.

With that, Shane returned to his vehicle, turned the

flashing lights on, and pulled out in front of Kade. They flew the rest of the way to the lodge.

Kade parked and jumped out of his car. He quickly thanked Shane then took the steps of the lodge two at a time.

Asher opened the door and whistled in appreciation. "I guess I won't have to teach you how to arrive in style." He nodded toward the retreating police car. "Any chance you told him nothing?"

"He's a friend." Mouth dry, Kade asked, "How's Dale?"

Asher's expression was tight. "Resting. What did you tell him?"

"Shane? Does it matter right now?"

"What's his last name? I'll handle it."

"There's nothing to handle. I trust Shane."

"Trust. You'll get over that. Shane who?"

Asher blocking the door was symbolic, at least to Kade. He did want Asher's help, but that didn't negate what he knew about the people of Bright or himself. "Drop it, Asher. He is a friend. Don't let me hear that you so much as googled his name. If I go to Boston I'll follow your lead, but this is my town, my people, my rules. Now are you going to tell me what's going on with Dale or do I need to find someone else who will?"

Ian appeared behind him. "Is that Kade?" He took one look at Asher's face and asked, "What's wrong?"

Asher waved a dismissive hand. "Apparently nothing. He has everything under control."

Kade sighed.

Asher stepped back to let Kade in. "Dad's going to be

fine. He accidentally double-dosed on his medication and got light-headed. We're watching him, but the doctor said as long as there is no change he's fine to remain here."

Relief flooded in. "Good." There was no need to hide it from them. "What's the medication for?"

Ian closed the door behind them. "We think it's stress. He's been losing weight, battling mild angina. We finally convinced him to see a cardiac specialist back home. He was fine until we started looking for you . . ."

Asher shook his head at Ian. "And people say I have no tact. Kade, welcome to scared Ian. He found Dad on the floor this morning. He's still rattled."

Kade felt a wave of sympathy for them both. They were all going through this together. "I'm pretty rattled myself. I meant to talk to Dale yesterday but the timing was never right."

The three of them walked into the foyer, shoulder to shoulder. Lance and Grant joined them. Grant said, "Kade's here. Good. Dad's looking more alert."

Kade glanced around. "Where's Sophie?"

Lance answered, "With Willa and the twins. The women are all trying to keep Mom's mind off how Dad is doing, but she's holding up better than the rest of us. She'll be glad you're here, Kade."

"No Annie today?" Grant asked.

"Working," Kade answered automatically.

Andrew joined the group. "Dad suggested we don't tell Kade, but I'm guessing it's too late for that."

Kade tensed. "If my being here is going to add any stress,

I can go—"

"No," several of his brothers said in unison.

Grant gave Kade a sympathetic pat on the back. "You belong here. That's your father in there too. You should go in."

After a moment, Kade squared his shoulders. He scanned the faces of his brothers. Andrew was a tough read. Asher *seemed* unaffected, but Kade now knew it was all show. Ian was quieter than normal. Lance looked concerned. Grant was composed but ready to jump into action if called upon.

My brothers.

"I'll keep my visit short," Kade promised.

Andrew stepped closer and in a low tone, he said, "Take your time, Kade. We can't help him. You're what he needs right now."

"Thanks, Andrew." Kade smiled.

Without smiling back, Andrew walked off.

Kade stood there, momentarily at a loss for how to react. Lance offered more confusing advice. "One relationship at a time, Kade. Go see Dad."

Because there's an issue with Andrew? I don't even know him.

Shaking off the questions he had regarding the brother he'd originally thought he'd bond the best with, Kade followed Grant to the door of his father's room. Grant opened the door to a suite then left him.

Kade took a deep breath and stepped inside.

DURING THE DOWNTIME between flying one client to

Melbourne and another one back, Annie texted her friend Claire to see if she was free for lunch. Like Annie, Claire was a small business owner. Annie joked that the love of telling people what to do had been the seed of inspiration for Claire's Accountability Coaching Agency. Whatever the truth was, there was no denying the success Claire had found by relocating to Melbourne. Her client list included actors, business owners, and even some politicians—many of whom were also Annie's clients.

Claire was already seated at a table in their favorite central business district restaurant. Of course it was vegan and gluten-free friendly—Claire wouldn't have it any other way. Tall and thin with long, straight brown hair that was always done up in the latest style, if one didn't know Claire they'd think fashion and fitness came easy to her. The truth was she'd fought and won against a good number of challenges. Born to a single, financially strapped mother, Claire had been heavy well into her late teens. Dedication to exercising and nutritional discipline had given her a body swimsuit models would envy. Grit and confidence had put her in the top of Melbourne's social circle. She was her own poster child for success.

That day, however, she was simply Claire—one of Annie's best friends and a much-needed sounding board. Annie hugged her then took a seat across from her. They ordered iced matcha tea lattes and smashed avocado on toast with a side of tomatoes and almond feta cheese.

"What time do you fly back?" Claire asked after the waitress walked away.

"Four. I'll have time to hit the gym and shower. I need it." She accepted her latte from the waitress and held it up in Claire's direction. "I don't eat like this without you."

"You should." Claire sipped on her own drink before answering. "You're lucky you've never needed to, but you might want to cut down on the chips for the sake of your heart if not your waist."

"Yes, Mum," Annie said with a smile. "Speaking of doing something that might not be in my best interests . . ."

"You didn't sleep with one of your clients, did you?"

"When have I ever done that?" When Claire opened her mouth to cite the time, Annie raised her hand to stop her. "One time. It was one time, and I learned my lesson. This is totally different."

Claire wrinkled her nose. "Not one of *my* clients?"

"No. Relax. I'd never do that to you."

"I know, but you look so guilty. I can't think of what would put that expression on your face."

"Kade is back in Bright."

Claire shook her head and covered her eyes briefly with one hand. The waitress interrupted to deliver their food. Claire waited until she was gone before saying, "I thought you were over him."

Annie grimaced and shrugged. "Over-ish?"

Claire unrolled her cutlery from her napkin. "Before I say anything, what are you looking for from me? Do you want me to have an opinion or just listen? I can't control any twitches I may develop, but I'll hold my silence if you need me to."

That's a good friend. "You probably couldn't say anything worse than what I've been telling myself, so no need to hold back. Plus, I value your advice, even if I decide not to take it."

"Fair enough. So, Kade is back. Did he ask you out?"

"It's so much more complicated than that," Annie said then stuck her fork through a succulent little tomato and popped it into her mouth. After chewing it, she said, "You have to swear to keep this between us. Hold your questions until the end, because it's a wild tale that you need to hear in its entirety."

Claire paused while cutting into her salad. "It's in the vault, but start talking because I only have an hour for lunch and you've piqued my interest."

Annie hadn't said anything to anyone in Bright, but she and Claire had always told each other everything. There was no way to update Claire on her own life without bringing her up to speed on Kade's as well. Annie started with the shock of seeing him in her family's pub and didn't hold back how she'd felt when she did. She walked Claire through the emotional dinner at her parents' when Kade had told them about the Barringtons and how her father had suggested Annie go with him to meet them.

From there, the rest of the story flowed—right down to waking up in Kade's arms that morning. Before saying anything, Claire did a quick search on her phone, then turned it for Annie to see. "These Barringtons?"

Annie scanned the photo. "That's them."

"Holy shit. That's the family you want to find you. But

still, I can't even imagine how I'd deal."

"Kade is struggling. So are they. But they seem like they want the best for him."

"You picked a hell of a time to sleep with Kade."

"I know."

"He has to be freaking out about all of this."

"He is."

Claire laid her utensils down and held Annie's gaze. "Have you considered he might be using you as a source of comfort during a tough time?"

I need to hear this. "I have."

"Does he know how you feel about him?"

"No, not really."

Claire pursed her lips, looking suddenly sad. "I don't see this going anywhere good, Annie. You're going to get your heart broken and he . . . he's going to leave you again. From what you've said, the Barringtons came for their son. He's going back to Boston with them whether he knows it or not yet. Then what?"

Annie stabbed her fork through a clump of cheese. "I don't know. I'm trying not to think about that. It doesn't feel wrong to be with him, Claire. It feels so right. He's here at least until Viviana and Grant get married next weekend. Not every relationship lasts. If I go into this knowing it probably won't—but it'll be good while it does—is that so wrong?"

Claire sighed. "Not wrong, but it's an unhealthy pattern for you. I was there when you waited for him to come back after college. Then after he moved to Wabonga. I commiserated with you when you finally realized he wasn't coming back. He's like an addiction to you, and you're better when you cut him completely out of your life."

Tapping her fingers on the table, Annie processed the truth in Claire's words. "He needs me," she countered.

"He doesn't," Claire said with a sympathetic expression. "He's a grown man. Maybe he was in shock at first, but that passes. I've known Kade as long as you have. He's no pushover. He'll be fine."

Clasping her hands on the table, Annie dug deeper. "I want this time with him more than I care how much it might hurt to lose him later."

"Does that sound like a healthy choice to you?"

Annie took her time before grudgingly admitting, "No, it doesn't."

Claire reached over and took Annie's hands in hers. "I'm not saying anything you don't already know. He's confused, not sure what he feels about anything, and he was honest about that. Those are your words, not mine."

"I lied to him about how I feel. I'm having a hard time dealing with that."

"Because you are one of the kindest, most honest people I know. Don't settle for what he offers while he's in crisis. You can be there for him and not be his comfort fuck."

"Ouch." Tough love was, well, tough to hear. "What do I do? Just go back and tell him the sex was great but we need to close that door?" *Please don't say yes.*

Claire nodded. "That sounds exactly like what you should say."

Annie took a shaky breath. "And then it's over."

"Maybe, but I know you, Annie, and you'll be okay. You don't need him. You've not only survived without him—you've thrived. Don't undervalue yourself. Tour guide or billionaire, he couldn't find a better partner than you'd be. If he doesn't see that, he doesn't deserve you. You were there for him, now be there for you. If he's really the man you think he is, he'll come around. If he doesn't, consider yourself a Kade-aholic and take it one day at time."

"Kade-aholic." Annie smiled. "How much do I owe you for this therapy session?"

"One week off sugar."

Annie's jaw fell in horror. "None?"

"You'll feel better."

"Or kill someone," Annie grumbled. "I love my coffee sweet."

Claire shrugged. "I can't make you give it up, but you did ask."

"I did." Annie sucked down a good portion of her green latte. "No sex. No sugar. It's going to be a long week."

Claire laughed. "You'll live, and one day you might even thank me."

She shouldn't have to wait. "I am grateful. I needed this talk. I was regressing to high school-Annie and felt like I couldn't control it."

Claire took a delicate bite of her salad, chewed it slowly, then said, "Everyone feels like that sometimes. I call it job security. I have this conversation ten times a day with people you'd never think would doubt themselves."

"All Kade-aholics?" Annie joked.

"Sure." Claire rolled her eyes and chuckled. She sobered and asked, "So, are any of the Barringtons in need of my services?"

"Every last one of them," Annie quipped. "Honestly, they're in a rough spot, but I like them. I offered to give them a tour. Should I say I can't?"

"I don't see any harm in being nice to Kade's family as long as you don't fuck any of *them*."

Annie burst out laughing. "And people say I'm blunt."

"Birds of a feather, baby. Birds of a feather." She raised her glass. "To strong, independent women."

They clinked glasses. "And to good friends." She finished her drink, then asked, "So, how is your love life?"

Claire made a face and leaned in. "Let me run a scenario by you, and you tell me what you think . . ."

And that was why their friendship had endured. Claire had no trouble giving advice, but she didn't hide that she was also human and flawed. Their hour lunch went well over, but Claire didn't balk. There were some things that were worth rearranging one's schedule for, and friendship was one of them.

On her walk to the gym, Annie received a text from Kade.

Dinner tonight?

She answered: **Long day, but you can call me around nine.**

Kade: **Call? Like phone?**

Annie: **Yes, if you have time.**

Kade: **Is everything okay?**

Annie: **Yes, but I do want to talk.**
Kade: **I can come over.**

She grimaced. It would have been so easy to say yes. She wasn't ready to tell him how she felt about him, but she also didn't want to lie to him anymore. **Then we won't talk.**

He didn't immediately answer, but eventually texted, **I'll call you at nine.**

Annie continued to the gym that was often a home away from home for her. Buoyed by her conversation with Claire, she felt better than she had in a long time. Yes, she'd slept with Kade. Yes, she still had feelings for him.

I'm no one's comfort fuck. Not even his.

Tonight I'll find a nice way to tell him that.

And we'll go from there.

Chapter Twelve

THAT NIGHT, KADE pulled his car up to the lake where he and Annie had spent so much time when they were younger. He left his car running and looked out over the water by the illumination of the headlights. He was exhausted from another emotional day with the Barringtons. Selfishly, all he wanted to do was lose himself in Annie's arms and her bed.

He glanced at his watch. Almost time to call her.

Call—not see. He'd expected the day to end much differently. It had started with shower sex worthy of a porn movie. The taste of her was still on his lips. His pants tented as he remembered digging his hands into her hair when she sank to her knees and took him deep in her mouth. God, she was perfect. He loved the little sounds she made when she came and how she wrapped around him while he fucked her in the bed, on the floor, and against the wall of the shower.

He ached from the raw need to have her again.

Not tonight, though.

Tonight she wanted to *talk*.

Talking was what he'd done all day. He'd talked to Dale

about his health and his guilt. He'd talked to Sophie about how Dale needed to see Kade's life for himself—how he needed to bear witness to the good life he'd had despite how it had started.

He talked to Kenzi about Andrew's struggle with drugs and his own journey back to the family. Then he attempted to talk to Andrew—something that was never well received. There was something with Andrew, some unspoken issue that no one would admit to, that strained every interaction with him. Kade wished someone would tell him whatever it was, but so far no one would.

After leaving Lavender Farm, Kade had talked to his parents at length about Dale's health and what it was like to spend time with his biological family. His mother was almost ready to meet Sophie. They'd talked about that as well.

Talk. Talk. Talk.

Kade would have liked nothing more than to retreat into the mountains for a week to defrag, but his time with the Barringtons was just beginning. They wanted to see the area, meet his friends, include him in the wedding plans.

And talk more about his inheritance and all the legal ramifications of accepting it.

Kade checked the time on his phone again. Finally. He chose Annie's number and sighed as it rang. He didn't want to talk about anything else, but he wanted to know if Annie was upset about something. Whatever it was, he'd make it right.

"Kade."

He loved the way she said his name, loved it even more

when she cried it out as she climaxed or while begging him not to stop doing whatever was driving her wild. He shook his head, bringing his focus back to the present. "How was your day?"

"Good. I spent most of it in Melbourne. Had lunch with Claire. Do you remember her?"

"Of course I do. How is she?"

"As amazing as always. She's doing really well there."

"That's good to hear."

"How about you?"

"I spent it at the lodge with . . . my. . . the Barringtons."

"Oh, that's great. Is it getting easier?"

"For the most part. I don't know that I'll ever have much in common with them, but it's definitely getting better. Today I had a long conversation with Dale. You were right—he has a lot of guilt. I'm hoping I can help him let some of that go."

"You will. He lucked out with you as a son. When he realizes that, the past won't matter as much."

Kade nodded. "That's pretty much what Sophie said."

Neither of them said anything for a few long moments. There was definitely something weighing on Annie's mind so Kade waited. Eventually, she said, "Kade, these past few days have been incredible."

No. No. No.

"But?"

"You need time to get to know your family."

"Trust me, I have enough time with them."

"And I need to place my focus back on my business. This

is a hectic time of year for me. I have trainees waiting for me to walk them through our program, and it's a lot on my plate."

"What are you saying, Annie?" In his head the question sounded concerned, but it came out in an irritated tone. "Do you want to end it?"

She let out an audible breath. "I can't sleep with you anymore, Kade. It's not fair to me, and it's not fair to you. If you want to talk I'm still here for you. I care, but I can't do this."

"*Talk?* No thanks, I've had my fill of that." As soon as it was voiced, he regretted it. He knew he sounded like an ass, but he was angry. How could she ditch him when he needed her most?

Her voice was tight like she was holding back tears, and he felt even worse. She said, "Okay, then. I won't keep you on the phone; I just wanted to be upfront about what I need."

"What about what I need?" Kade growled. No, it wasn't fair, but it was how he felt.

In a gentle tone, she said, "It's always been about that, Kade, but that's never worked out for us. I want to be there for you, but I can't *be there* for you anymore. I'm sorry." With that, she hung up.

He went to call her back, apologize, grovel, demand she change her mind . . . something. Instead he cursed and threw the phone on the seat beside him.

WITH A SHAKING hand, Annie attached her phone to the

charger and placed it carefully on her bedside table. She'd done it. She'd ended it.

The sex had been fucking amazing. She was certain all it would take to have him beside her that night was a text saying she'd changed her mind. But then what? Seeing him like an addiction had given Annie the clarity she'd never had with him.

Chasing him, hanging on his every word as if his next would be a declaration of love for her, was an unhealthy pattern. She could hate herself for those moments of weakness, or she could move forward making better choices.

Like Claire always says—it's my life, my choice.

She walked to the kitchen and took out a container of her favorite cookies. Each and every one of them begged to be dunked in a glass of milk and promised to make her temporarily feel better. *No.* She dumped the container in the trash then filled a bowl with carrot slices instead.

She plopped down on the couch and bit into a piece of carrot. Like every man she'd slept with besides Kade, it didn't live up to what she craved. *But it's better for me.* She chomped down on another piece.

She blindly surfed through the channels on her television. None held her attention. She turned the television off and decided sleep was her best option for escape.

Her phone beeped from an incoming message. Her stomach flipped nervously. What if it was Kade? Was she strong enough to refuse him if he persisted?

She checked her phone.

Kenzi: You up?

Annie: Hi.

Kenzi: I was wondering if you know of a nice place that does high tea. I'd like to surprise Viviana with that and a shopping trip before her wedding.

Annie: Sounds like you want to head to Melbourne. I can get you the names of some places with good reviews.

Kenzi: Any chance you have time to take us? We'd hire you, of course. It'd be a day trip for the women only. Eight of us. Do you have a helicopter big enough for all of us?

Annie: I do, but it'll be a little crowded. And you're not hiring me. I promised you a tour.

Kenzi: If you're sure. We'd love to include you the whole day. Also, if you want to bring someone along, we'd love to meet your friends as well.

Interesting. *Annie:* One of my best friends lives and works in Melbourne. I can ask her if she's free. When would you want to go?

Kenzi: When could you take us?

Annie pulled up her online schedule for her fleet. The larger, luxury copter was open the next day. She'd have to get coverage for two of her own runs, but she did have a couple of employees looking for more hours.

Annie: Tomorrow? Do you want me to see if there are openings at the places I know?

Kenzi: Tomorrow would be perfect. Send me the info and I'll contact them.

That made sense. Who would refuse the Barringtons? There was a buzz even among her clients regarding the American family being somewhere in the Victoria region. Annie's pilots were being asked if they'd seen them, knew who they might be connected with. Being seen with them in public would only make it worse.

She texted the names of a few tea rooms to Kenzi while debating if she should have one of her other pilots take the ladies to Melbourne.

She liked them, but they were Kade's family. Was Kenzi only reaching out to her because she thought Annie and Kade were dating?

Annie: **There's something you should know before we go tomorrow.**

Kenzi: **Yes?**

Annie: **Kade and I are just friends. And we've hit a rocky spot. He may not want me to hang out with his family.**

Kenzi: **The best way to make it down a rocky road is to just keep going. You and Kade looked like you care about each other too much to let whatever happened stay a problem.**

We do and who knows? *Maybe there is a way back to friendship for us.*

Annie: **Okay. Then I'll clear my schedule for tomorrow. What time would you like to be picked up? I can land right on the lodge lawn.**

Kenzi: **Let's leave at eleven.**

Annie: **I'm not up on the best places to shop, but Claire will be.**

Kenzi: **Fantastic. Can't wait to meet her.**

Annie texted Claire. **I know you're busy, but would you have time to meet the Barrington women tomorrow? I'm taking them into Melbourne for high tea and shopping.**

Claire: **Hell yes, I'm in. What time?**

Annie: **We're leaving Bright at eleven. I told them you'd know the best shops.**

Claire: **I certainly do. Want me to arrange everything on this side?**

Annie: **No need. Kenzi is calling for the reservation for tea. Then just shopping.**

Claire: **You're so cute. There is no just shopping for people like the Barringtons. I'll call around and have some boutiques prepare for them.**

Annie: **Prepare?**

Claire: **Oh, hon. You have no idea. Which one did you say was getting married while here?**

Annie: **Viviana.**

Claire: **What do you know about her?**

Annie told her what Viviana had told her about her humble upbringing in the US.

Annie: **She did ask me if I could connect her with local vendors.**

Claire: **Trust me?**

Annie: **Absolutely.**

Claire: **Then pick me up on the top of the Sterling building. That never gets old. I'll arrange the rest.**

Annie laughed. **You got it. And thank you!**

Chapter Thirteen

KADE WOKE UP in a foul mood the next morning, and his day went downhill from there. He cut his jaw while shaving, backed his car into the stone wall that flanked one side of his parents' driveway, and received an emailed cancelation for a large tour group. Calling his Wabonga office didn't help. He'd left Todd, one of best guides, in charge. Apparently, right after Kade left, Todd caught his wife cheating on him, started going to the office drunk, and was managing to piss off every single person he encountered. His staff was refusing to go to work, his clients were not getting the tours they'd been promised, and no one had bothered to call him.

This is bullshit.

He parked in front of the lodge and called one of his MIA guides—no answer. Bile rose in his throat. His life felt like it was unraveling before his eyes.

There was a knock on his car window. He groaned when he saw who it was. Sorry, Viviana, I don't have the patience for meatheads right now. He left his window up and tried to make another call.

The passenger doors across and behind him opened then the two hulking men climbed in. Dylan said, "You have to save us, Kade. We are so fucking bored."

Connor leaned over the back of the seat. "He looks upset, Dylan."

Another door opened as Clay slid into the backseat with Connor. "Sorry, what are we doing?"

"You three are getting the fuck out of my car so I can have a minute to think," Kade snapped.

Dylan scratched the back of his neck. "He does look pissy."

"What's wrong, Kade?" Dylan asked as if he were the one Kade would turn to for help.

"Nothing. Everything," Kade growled, running both hands through his hair before slamming them on the steering wheel.

Clay addressed the meatheads as if Kade couldn't hear him. "It's been a long week for him. Let me handle this."

He glared at Clay. "Get the hell away from me."

In a smooth, cocky tone, that made Kade want to sock him in the face, Clay said, "We're here for you, Kade. What do you need?"

Kade closed his eyes, rubbing his hands over them. "It's all going to shit anyway. Why not?" He told them about what he'd learned was going on at his office.

Clay's face lit up. "Trouble with your adventure tour company? I'd love to help you with that."

Kade frowned. Clay didn't look like the outdoorsy type at all. "Have you ever even been paragliding? White water rafting?" As Clay simply stared back at him, Kade continued, "Camping?"

Clay shrugged and shook his head.

Connor jumped in the backseat, bouncing the whole vehicle as he did. "Oh, my God, yes. I want to do all of it. Right now. Today. Let's go."

Dylan snorted. "Idiot, he's not asking us if we want to do it, he's asking Clay if he's qualified to take someone on those tours."

"Clay could take us." Connor swatted Dylan in the back of his head. "Come on, Clay, I can't play another game of chess with Asher. He scares me. Let's go touring."

"I'm in," Clay said. "Lexi will understand. I can fly out this morning."

Kade waved a hand. "It's not that easy. My office is in chaos. I have disgruntled clients, no tour guides, and a drunk office manager."

Clay's smile widened. "Stop. You had me at *chaos*."

"No," Kade said. "This is my company. My problems. I'll fix them."

Connor slumped in his seat. "I knew it was too good to be true."

"You give up too easily," Clay assured the man. "Consider me your business's fairy godmother."

Dylan and Connor exchanged a confused look.

"Of sorts," Clay continued. "Listen, you have enough on your plate here. Let me take over your business for a few days. If I lose someone—I'll try to make it one of them." He thumbed toward Viviana's brothers.

"Please," Connor begged.

"We'll never survive another week here," Dylan whined.

The way things were going, Clay probably couldn't make it worse. I can't believe I'm considering this. "Be nice to Todd. He's usually a solid guy."

"I'll fly in some models. He'll forget all about his cheating wife," Clay assured him.

"You can do that?" Dylan asked, his jaw dropping open.

"He's joking," Kade said.

Clay mouthed, "I'm not."

"Lexi doesn't mind you hanging out with other women?" Connor asked.

Clay snapped his fingers. "Good point. I'll make the arrangements, but you two should retrieve the models from the airport and set them up in a hotel. Lexi is understanding, but not *that* understanding. Maybe we should skip the models."

"Your call," Connor said like a boy who had glimpsed a jar of cookies only to be told he couldn't have any of them.

Dylan shook it off. "We'll rescue Kade's company like the three musketeers would."

"It doesn't need to be *rescued*," Kade rushed to assure. "All I need is someone there making calls to get coverage. Maybe this isn't such a good idea."

Clay smoothed his ruffled clothing. "All joking aside, I'll have your office running smoothly and be back well before the wedding. I practically run Dax's company when he's away."

"Really?" It was difficult to imagine Dax handing the reins of his company to his eccentric friend. Dax had said, however, that Clay was a good one to have in his corner. So, maybe he was more responsible than he appeared. "Okay. Normally nothing would stop me from going back, but—"

"Say no more." Clay raised both hands. "Boys, pack your bags. This is going to be fun." With that, he stepped out of the car.

Dylan and Connor scrambled out of the car and sprinted into the lodge. Kade stepped out of the car and called to Clay.

Clay turned.

"My father started the tour company. It's important to me."

Looking serious for once, Clay nodded before walking up the steps of the lodge.

Kade stood beside his car, questioning the sanity of his decision. Under any other circumstances, he would have flown back to his office himself. For a long time nothing had been more important than its success. Today he wanted to see Dale on his feet, and if he was up to it, he wanted to show him around Bright.

He also wanted to hear from Annie, but so far he hadn't. He'd almost texted her a hundred times since their conversation the night before. He'd handled it badly and wanted to make sure she was okay. If that was all he wanted to say he would have sent that text. He wanted to tell her she was wrong. There was no reason they couldn't be together while he got to know his family.

She was right, though.

It wasn't fair to be with her while he didn't even know

his own fucking name. She was smart to call it off. If she'd ended up a casualty of this confusing time, he would never have forgiven himself.

It sucked though.

He'd fallen asleep with her on his mind.

Woke up remembering what it was like to wake up to her.

Showered without her.

Kenzi came flying down the steps with Dax at her side. He greeted her with a kiss to the cheek.

Dax said, "Kade, I spoke to Clay. Do you want me to call him off?"

Kade blanched. In comparison to everything else going on, did it really matter? He'd run damage control after the dust settled. "No, he's excited to help. I'm sure he has experience in all types of businesses."

Dax shrugged but didn't confirm nor deny that.

Kenzi turned at the sound of a helicopter landing on the lawn beside the lodge and rushed to meet it. Kade whistled at the size of it. Nothing but the best for the Barringtons. "Impressive."

Dax gave Kade an odd look. "It's Annie's. She's taking the ladies to Melbourne for a day of shopping."

"That's Annie's?" Kade looked the chopper over with fresh eyes. He'd known Annie was doing well and that she shuttled business people now, but she'd obviously come a very long way. His chest swelled with pride for her. "Good for her."

"Surprised? We were all under the impression you knew

Annie really well."

Without taking his eyes off the chopper, especially as the motor cut and Annie stepped out of it, Kade said, "We'd drifted out of each other's lives until I met her again when I came home to meet all of you."

"Interesting."

"Not really, I practically grew up at her house the same way she did at mine. When I felt like my life was being turned upside down, it made sense to talk to someone I could trust."

As soon as she cleared the blades, Annie straightened, looked up, and met his gaze. With a pained smile, she raised a hand in a curt wave then turned away to greet Kenzi and the women heading down the steps toward her.

His reaction to her arrival was complicated. Part of him wanted to rush over, pick her up, swing her around, and kiss her until they both forgot why she'd called it off. Part of him wanted to remind her that she was the one who said she didn't want to see him. If she wanted it to be over, what the hell was she doing with his family?

Dax cleared his throat. "Are you going to say hello?"

Kade pocketed his hands. "I don't want to make things awkward for her."

"I believe they already are," Dax said before stepping away to speak to Kenzi who was smiling and excited.

Kade pushed off and walked over to the enthusiastic group. Sophie gestured for him to come to her side. "Are you taking your father out today?" she asked for his ears only.

"Yeah, I thought I'd show him around Bright. Nothing

too far or too strenuous."

She glanced at the other ladies then back. "I hate to miss that."

"I can do it again tomorrow. It's not that big, but a little sunshine will be good for him."

Her face lit with a smile even as her eyes misted with tears. "There was a time when I didn't think I could ever be happy again. I did my best to go on, but a part me was missing. Every time I see you, I'm impressed with the man you've become, and I put more of that sadness behind me."

He didn't know what to say to that, so he simply hugged her and assured her he'd take good care of Dale. When he looked up he caught Annie watching him. She quickly turned away, but not before he saw longing in her eyes. Then why—why end it? Would he ever understand her?

He released Sophie and greeted the rest of the group and finally Annie. "Hey."

"Hey, yourself," she said with an overly bright smile.

He flicked his chin toward her helicopter. "It's good to see you doing so well. That's a real step up from what I remember you flying."

"Thanks." Her cheeks flushed. "My clients like to arrive in style."

He didn't like how little he actually knew about her present life or her clients. Were they all men? Was she in a relationship with any of them? Was that why she'd called it off with him? "Well, it looks like you certainly provide that for them."

She frowned at his tone. He felt like an arse because he

was being one, but he couldn't stop. He wanted to demand she forget about his family and go somewhere with him so they could talk. Funny that the last thing he'd wanted to do the night before felt imperative right then.

He needed to know why.

His brothers arrived, some with babies in hand, and there was a flurry of farewells. Annie assured them she'd have them back early. Willa joked, "Not too early. I see a mimosa or two in my future."

Everyone laughed.

"Ready?" Annie asked.

"Annie," Kade called out urgently when she turned away.

She stopped and turned back.

His mind went absolutely blank. For a moment there was only her and a primal desire to have her, to grab her close and not let her leave his side ever again. It didn't make sense, but it was undeniable. *I walked away from her once, how do I avoid losing her this time?* "Thanks for doing this for my family."

She nodded, shook her head, then turned away to lead the group onto the helicopter. Flanked by his brothers and their children, he watched her seamlessly take off and disappear over the treeline.

Ian spoke first. "Dad's almost ready. Do you want any of us to go with you?"

"No, we'll be fine. We're not going far." Both Asher and Grant had already walked Kade through all the possible things that could go wrong with Dale's condition and how to address each. He wasn't eager for round three.

Ian ran a hand across his forehead. "If he goes pale or sweaty or shaky—"

Grant broke in. "He knows."

"I just want to make sure if anything happens—"

"I have all of your numbers, the list of medications he's on, the list of medications he's allergic to, the phone number of the doctor who last treated him, as well as the contact information for his physician in the States." Kade stopped long enough to take a breath before adding, "I'm also trained in CPR as well as basic emergency medical procedures."

Juggling his two children on either hip, Lance joked, "That's more prepared than I'd be."

Asher cuddled his sleeping son against his chest. "We could send Andrew with them."

"No," Andrew said then turned on his heel and walked away. Looking concerned, Dax followed after him.

"Or not," Asher said with irony. Once Andrew was out of earshot, he added, "Kade, when you get back from taking Dad out, you might want to have a sit-down with Andrew. He's taking this harder than I thought he would."

Easier said than done. "I don't get what his problem is with me."

"You'll have to ask him," Asher said, soothing his child with a bounce or two when he stirred.

"I've tried," Kade insisted.

"You didn't try hard enough," Asher said in a low tone. "I'm heading in to put Joe down." Then he walked into the lodge.

Lance handed his daughter Wendy to Grant. "Willa just

fed them so I'll need a second set of hands soon, and you could use the practice."

"Wendy, you wouldn't make a mess for your uncle to clean, would you?" Grant raised the baby over his head, cooed, then brought her down for a quick nuzzle that made her laugh. "She says she'd never do that to me." He walked off with Lance and the infant.

It was a softer side to his brothers that was heartwarming to see. They might disagree, but they obviously cared about each other as well as their wives and children.

Alone with Ian, Kade rocked back on his heels. At first meet, Ian had come across as pompous and controlling. The more time Kade spent with him, though, the less happy he seemed. The rest of his siblings were paired up and starting their own families. Could that be his problem?

"You're welcome to come with us if you want to," Kade offered.

"No, all set." He motioned toward the lodge. "I have calls to make."

"What exactly do you do?"

Without blinking, Ian said, "I'd tell you, but then I'd have to kill you."

Kade chuckled until he realized Ian wasn't laughing along. "Right. Okay, then. I'll go get Dale."

Ian's expression tightened. "Could you do us all a favor and call him Dad? I get that you don't want to go by your old name, but I want to throw up every time I hear you call them Sophie and Dale. Not only are they your parents, but they've mourned you. They suffered while you clearly did not. It's time to make an effort to bring them peace."

Standing straighter in the face of Ian's criticism, Kade shook his head. "I hadn't realized I wasn't."

"The blood test came back positive. There's no denying you're Kent—"

"That's a relief," Kade countered with sarcasm.

"But I don't trust you. Who has your allegiance? The Barringtons or the Thompsons?"

What the hell? "Does it have to be one or the other?"

"One day it might. If that day comes, which family would you choose?"

"Why?"

Ian leaned in and in a dangerous, cold voice said, "Because I don't yet buy Pamela's version of what happened. For me, it's not enough that you're back. I'm looking into what happened that night, and you can tell your *mother* that if I discover she was involved in the plot to take you—I will make her pay dearly."

Ian strode off before Kade had a chance to assure him that Pamela's version was the truth, the only truth he could handle. "Good talk." He took several deep breaths. Part of him wanted to drag Ian back and warn him to stay away from his parents. Another part of him was tired of verbally sparring with his brothers. Kade wouldn't let anything happen to Pamela and Dave. They'd been too good to him for too long.

It was sad, though, to see he hadn't progressed as far with the Barringtons as he'd thought. Lately each step he took forward sent him two steps back.

Even with Annie.

What am I missing? How am I supposed to be handling this?

Deep in thought, he didn't realize Dale had joined him until he was standing at his side. "What's troubling you, Son?"

Kade met the older man's gaze. Calling him anything but Dale didn't feel right. He was still very much a stranger. "Nothing. Are you ready to go?"

Dale rubbed a shaking hand across his jaw. "I wasn't always this man. There was a time when I trusted my instincts. I believed I knew what was best for my family. My children are stubborn and proud because I have been. Everything that once made sense to me doesn't anymore."

Nodding, Kade said, "I understand that feeling well. Dale, I can't begin to know how my disappearance affected all of you, but it brought no harm to me. While you were mourning for me, I was happy. I don't know if I'm supposed to feel guilty about that or downplay it . . ."

Dale wiped a tear from the corner of one of his eyes. "You have nothing to feel guilty about, and I want to hear every happy memory you have. I haven't slept right since I first heard you might be alive. Endless unspeakable possibilities haunted me. To see you now, to know that Pamela brought you somewhere safe and raised you the way she did, to learn the kind of man you've become—you don't know what that means to me, to us."

It was an emotional moment for both of them. Kade was overcome by a need to comfort his biological father so he hugged him tightly, like a son would after a long time away from a parent. "We'll get through this," he assured Dale when he released him.

Dale sniffed and composed himself.

After a long pause, Kade asked, "Would you like to meet the man who raised me? I'm sure he's free, but I could text to confirm he'll be around."

After blinking a few times, Dale nodded. "I'd like that very much."

"Sophie said she didn't want to miss anything, but we could do that tomorrow. I could invite my mu—Pamela, too."

Placing a hand on Kade's arm, Dale said, "It doesn't bother me to hear you call her your mother. The more we get to know you, the more grateful we are to her. Sophie feels the same way."

That was a relief to hear. Hopefully, Ian would begin to see it the same way. "Then let's get our tour started."

They walked together to Kade's Ranger and climbed in, as Ian and Andrew watched from the lodge. Had they been there the whole time and witnessed the emotional exchange? *If so, I'm sure they'd say I handled it poorly.* Kade waved in farewell. Neither waved back. *Whatever.*

Kade thought Dale had missed the exchange, but halfway down the driveway he said, "Of all my children, I worry about those two the most. They keep everything bundled up inside. It's not healthy. On the other hand, no one ever has to wonder what Asher is thinking."

Kade coughed out a laugh. "So true."

"Grant lets it out in another way. He's a mother hen. When he asks to go over your stock investments with you, it's his way of taking care of you."

"I've heard that about him."

"Kenzi was my perfect little girl, but she had her own struggles along the way that she hid from us. Meeting Dax, though, brought out a strength in her that has been inspiring to watch bloom. I'm so proud of her. All of my children have chosen well with their partners."

"That definitely has been my impression."

"We almost lost Andrew, but Helene brought him back from a dark place. Whatever else you hear about her or her family, she's one of the best things that has ever happened to ours."

Without looking away from the road, Kade frowned. "I'll keep that in mind." Where was he going with this? It felt like he was leading toward something.

"Andrew would be lost without her and her parents. They gave him something he didn't find with us—his purpose. I've never seen him happier than with her working on their large animal rescue in Florida. If he comes across as cold, he's not. He's afraid."

"Of what?"

When Dale didn't answer, Kade said, "I know. That's for him to tell me. Hopefully he decides to one day." His hands gripped the steering wheel tightly. "Do you have a suggestion about how to reach Ian?"

"Ian's a tough one. He's the one the others call when they need rescuing—even Asher. That's a heavy weight to carry. What is he saying?"

"Nothing in particular." Although it was tempting to vent his anger about how Ian had threatened Pamela, Kade didn't. Dale didn't need the stress, and Kade wasn't afraid of Ian. If he came for anyone Kade cared about, he would kick his arse all the way back to Boston.

Kade glanced at Dale and saw him watching him. "It's hard to pin down which of your brothers you remind me the most of. You've got an easygoing side that reminds me of Lance. Every now and then, though, you get a look in your eye that reminds me of Asher."

Kade smiled at the thought. "I'll take both comparisons as a compliment."

"You should. You've also worked hard to provide financially for Dave and Pamela the same way Grant would."

"Does he really know where everyone's money is?"

Dale chuckled. "Everyone except Ian."

That doesn't surprise me. Kade parked in front of a large glass and brick building with a playground and several sports fields. "That's the school I went to, which has kindergarten to year twelve. Less than five hundred students total. Everyone knew everyone—which was a blessing and a curse." He pulled back out onto the road. "Life here is slower than you'd find in Melbourne. People open their gardens to their neighbors and call it a festival. We'll celebrate almost anything. In fact, if we're not biking somewhere, hiking up some mountain to paraglide down, we're either fishing or kicking back a beer with friends. If more than ten people gather we call it an event. Hell, it might even make the town calendar."

"Sounds like it was a fine place to grow up."

"It really was." He pulled into the parking lot of a splash park near a river, bustling with children and adults. "Family and community are big here. We all played in the same places. People watched each other's children as closely as they watched their own. It drove me crazy when I was young. I couldn't sneeze in the park without my mother asking me if I was sick when I got home because someone called her."

"Did you miss that when you moved away?"

"I did. I enjoyed the challenge and felt like I was doing something important, but when I decide to settle down, it'll be here." He'd been sharing his gut feelings without thinking of how it might make Dale feel, but when he heard his own declaration, he stopped.

Dale asked, "So, you see yourself married with children?"

"One day." A frazzled-looking couple walking with a stroller spotted Kade and waved. He waved back. "Maybe not as many as they have. That's Anton and his high school crush, Kira. Every time I see them they have a new baby, so we joke they are single-handedly trying to double the population of Bright. Half the kids in that splash park are probably theirs. I used to know all their names, but I can't keep up."

Dale was smiling and looked relaxed. He seemed to be enjoying the area so much, Kade asked him if he wanted to get out and walk around. He said he did.

They walked into the splash park to meet Anton and Kira—as well as their herd. Kade enjoyed catching up with them. The only awkward moment was when Kade introduced Dale. He wasn't going to say much, but found himself announcing, "This is Dale, from my American side."

"No idea you had that side," Anton commented with very little curiosity. His attention was on his four-year-old who was picking up a stick to reprimand her little brother with. Anton trotted over to intervene.

He was back a moment later and conversation about local events flowed easily. Anton inquired about business in Wabonga and the health of Kade's parents. Kade caught up on Anton's renovations on the town's movie theater. It had been the buzz of the town when Anton had purchased it with plans of modernizing it. He joked that after a few days of picketing, mainly by a retired schoolteacher, Mrs. Simms, and her sisters, everyone adjusted to the idea of more comfortable seating and a better screen.

Kade thought about what he'd said to Dale about wanting to eventually settle in Bright. It wasn't just the town that was the lure. Annie was there. When he tried to imagine himself moving back to the area with another woman, he couldn't. Annie was home to him just like Bright was. A part of him had always known he'd come back to her. He'd never realized it until now.

More locals recognized Kade and came over with their children to catch up, returning his attention to the present. Dale smiled through meeting each and every one of them and was still smiling when Kade texted his father to meet them for lunch. "If you're okay with a brewery, we can head to the one Annie's parents own. Harrison will introduce you to anyone in town you haven't already met."

Dale nodded. Once back in the car, he gripped Kade's arm tightly. Kade froze, instantly concerned that he wasn't feeling well.

Dale's eyes were misty again. "I can't thank you enough for today, Kade. This was exactly what I needed."

Kade gave Dale's hand a pat. "I'm glad. Now let's eat. I'm starving."

Lunch went smoothly, as Kade had expected. His father and Dale bonded over everything from sports to health scares. Dale shared stories of his childhood and life in the US, but the focus was on happy times. Harrison was surprisingly quiet. Not at all how Kade expected him to be.

It wasn't a good sign as far as Annie went. Had Annie spoken to her brother about them?

Two hours passed surprisingly fast, and Kade looked back and forth between the two older men. They had more in common than he expected them to. They both loved their wives. Family was their priority. Neither believed in holding grudges. If not separated by thousands of miles and a substantial financial status gap, they might easily have been friends. Dale made sure Dave knew he would be missed if he didn't attend Grant and Viviana's upcoming wedding. Dave assured him they would be there. It was a nice exchange to watch.

Soon after that Dave had Dale chuckling over a story of something Kade had done as a child. Dale followed with a story of his sons doing something similar. His sons. *My brothers.* It still took him by surprise to think of them that way.

"I only had one child," Dave said, "but it often felt like I had three. Kade, Harrison, and Annie were inseparable as children. If you wanted to locate one, all you had to do was listen for the others."

Dale took a sip of his water before saying, "The whole family already adores Annie. In fact, she flew the ladies to Melbourne for a day of sightseeing and shopping."

"They're in good hands. Annie's a pro," his father answered, before pinning Kade with a look that said he knew things weren't going well with her. "How is she?"

"Not now, Dad," Kade hedged.

Dale didn't say anything, but his eyebrows rose and fell.

Dave made a pained face and lowered his voice. "One day Kade is going to wake up and marry that girl, if she doesn't find someone else before he comes to his senses."

"They do make a nice couple," Dale said while watching Kade's expression.

Kade excused himself to pay the bill then said, "This has been great, but I'm sure Dale would like to see more of the town before we head back to the lodge."

Dave shook Dale's hand. "That's my cue to go. It was very nice to meet you, Dale."

Both men stood. Dale said, "If you and Pamela have the time tomorrow, I'd love for you both to meet Sophie as well."

"You're on," Dave said with a smile and strong handshake.

A short time later, while they were driving through another section of Bright, Dale said, "I really enjoyed meeting

Dave. I see a lot of him in you. He's a good man."

"Yes, he is. I don't know how to wrap my head around not actually being his."

Dale cleared his throat. "You are his—in every way that matters. I hope one day you'll be able to see yourself as mine as well. Don't ever feel you have to choose. That's not what love or family is about."

If only all of the Barringtons felt that way.

"That means a lot to me, thanks." It was Kade's turn to wipe moisture from the corner of his eyes. He sure as hell hoped that was how this all worked out. He wasn't a praying man, but he sent up a plea that all Ian uncovered was confirmation of Pamela's version of her involvement. He didn't want to choose—couldn't imagine it not destroying him.

LATE IN THE afternoon, Annie landed her helicopter gently on the side lawn of the lodge and cut the engine. At a safe distance, laden with the Barringtons' purchases of the day, a second chopper from her fleet landed. The day couldn't have gone better, mostly due to Claire's experienced organizational skills. The top shops in Melbourne had closed their doors to other customers so the Barringtons could sip champagne and be catered to.

It was a productive day. Viviana found her dress, met with a wedding planner, and ordered everything needed for her upcoming ceremony. The other ladies bought clothing and some jewelry for the wedding.

Annie's business brought her into contact with successful

people on a daily basis, but shopping with billionaires had shown her a whole new level of elite. Every need was anticipated and addressed without ever being voiced. Claire told her that within minutes of mentioning the Barrington name, her phone had begun to ring with requests from people in her network who wanted to invite the family to an event. She'd never seen anything quite like it, not even with her high-profile clients. Of course, Claire hadn't shared the Barrington itinerary with any of them or even brought up those invites to the family. She was too savvy for that.

When they'd dropped Claire off at the top of the Sterling building, Sophie had asked Annie to cut the engine. She surprised Annie by following Claire onto the helipad to hug her and thank her for arranging such a perfect outing. The other ladies had followed suit. Their gratitude was sincere, and that impressed Annie. They hadn't allowed wealth to make them stuffy or entitled.

Many of the women had come from modest means, but Annie knew a change in financial status could quickly change a person. Somehow this family had remained grounded— almost humble. Willa's twin sister, Lexi, was perhaps the most extravagant of the group, but she made it look fun. Why have money if you weren't going to spend it? She surprised Annie, though, when at the end of her spree she asked if there was a local charity she could donate to. Claire made arrangements for that to happen without seeming at all surprised by the request. *Why bother to buy anything at all?* Annie would have asked, but Claire handled the request as if it were completely normal.

When the blades stopped, Annie headed to open the rear door of the helicopter. The men were already on their way across the lawn to meet them.

Sophie took both of Annie's hands in hers. "Thank you for the most incredible day. I hope we see more of your friend Claire. She was a joy to get to know."

Annie leaned forward to give Sophie a kiss on the cheek. "I'll tell her you said that. It'll make her day."

Kenzi hugged Annie next. "Seriously, what a perfect day. Thank you, Annie."

Viviana was smiling, but she looked tired as she thanked Annie. Willa and Lexi were laughing as they tag-team embraced Annie. Helene and her mother thanked Annie with the same sweet smiles. Emily dove in for her own hug. "We'll never forget today. What a great memory."

"It's no wonder your business is doing so well, Annie," Sophie gushed.

Annie was still basking in that praise when she spotted Kade striding toward them. Her throat tightened, and she swayed on her feet. For a moment it had felt as if she belonged there, as if she were a part of this group. Reminding herself that she wasn't, stung.

Kade walked right up, taking his place beside her as if he belonged there. The women moved off to greet their men and fill them in on how the day had gone.

Lexi paused to ask Kade, "Have you heard from Clay? He hasn't been answering my texts."

"No, sorry." With all that had gone on, Kade had forgotten Clay had headed to Wabonga. "He might be in an area without phone service. That's common up there. I'll call my office in a few and have him jump on a landline."

"Poor cell coverage is what I figured. I'm going to head in, but text me if you hear anything."

"Will do," Kade assured her.

Then it was just Kade and Annie standing beside her helicopter. Annie hoped she looked more composed than she felt. "I brought them all back safe and sound, so I'm ready to call this day a success." She searched Kade's face. "How was your day?"

"Good. Good. I showed Dale around and introduced him to some of the locals."

"That's nice."

"We had lunch at your family's pub. Dad met us."

"How did that go?"

"Better than expected. They got on really well."

"That's awesome." She clasped her hands to stop from throwing herself in his arms. If there were any chance they could make their way back to normal, she'd have to be stronger.

It wasn't easy, though. In the past she may have yearned for his kiss, but she hadn't known the pleasure of it. Her body had warmed at his nearness, but now it craved him with an intensity that made it difficult to think of much else. She could remember every kiss he'd trailed across her skin, every touch of his hand, every thrust of his cock. Her body flushed as desire licked through it.

Every time her eyes met his, she saw the same hunger burning within him. It wasn't enough to be wanted by him, though. Not anymore. She'd thought she could do the friends-with-benefits thing, even told him she was fine with it—but she knew she couldn't. Her heart was all or nothing when it came to him. She needed to break away from him again.

I didn't have to be here today. I didn't have to torture myself this way.

But I needed to know if I could see him and not be miserable.

I can't. At least not yet. This hurts too much.

That realization saddened her, but it also gave her the path she needed to take—one that didn't include him for a while, or possibly ever.

He groaned. "Annie, I hate this . . . I feel like I can't hug you to me. Could we—?"

"Not yet." She didn't give herself time to wonder what he might ask and disappoint her by not saying what she wanted to hear. "I have to go, Kade."

"Oh, I'd hoped you'd stay for dinner."

"I can't."

He reached for her but she took a step back. "Annie, don't do this. Stay. I'm sorry about what I said the other night. We do have things we should talk out."

Annie's stomach clenched, and she feared she was about to be sick at his feet. "I can't do this." She took another step back. "Do you think I want to be like this? I don't. I want to be casual and sophisticated, but I'm not. I've never been. You said you didn't want to see me hurt. Well, I'm hurting." He stepped closer, and she moved farther away. "I did it to myself, but that doesn't make it hurt any less. Do me a favor, Kade, and stay away from me for a bit. I need time."

"Time for what?" he demanded, grabbing her arm when she would have turned away.

She pulled her arm free. "I'm sorry, Kade. I don't know if telling you would make it better or worse, and I can't take that risk." She spun and rushed to her chopper, starting it up immediately. He backed away from the dust the rotors kicked up. She'd never forget the expression on his face. He looked as miserable as she felt, and she hated she was the reason.

It's not his fault, has never been his fault.

I'm sorry, Kade.

She pulled up and flew off without looking back. She didn't let herself shed a tear. Been there, done that. Claire was right—she was better without him. She didn't want it to be all or nothing. She loved him, not only as a mate, but also as a person. If she were stronger he would always have a place in her life. She'd find a way to be happy for him when he eventually found a wife. Her children would be friends with his.

But I can't do that.

You'd think by now this would have gotten easier.

Later that day, she walked into her family's pub. There were customers seated at tables but none at the bar, so that's where she sat. Harrison offered her a beer that she declined, then a wine that she also refused. When he pushed a ginger ale with grenadine and a cherry beneath her nose, she smiled sadly at it. Her father had started serving her Shirley Temples as a treat when she was a young girl. He'd claimed it could cure a scraped knee, ease the pain of losing a pet, and when shared, even help end an argument with a best friend. When Harrison had once argued that no drink had magical powers, their father had said this one did as long as it was served with a kiss.

Harrison surprised Annie by leaning over the bar and planting a kiss on her forehead in the same way their father had done all those years ago. She chuckled and wiped the corners of her eyes. "God, you're getting sappy in your old age."

Harrison shrugged. "I'm not the one who's thirty."

"Touché."

"So, I'd ask you how today went, but you look like shit."

She balled her napkin and threw it at him. "Thanks for nothing."

"So he still has no clue?"

Annie took a long swig of her childhood drink. "Don't you think he has enough on his plate right now without me dropping that bombshell on him?"

Harrison bent to rinse a towel before wiping it across the bar. "I'd want to know."

"Well, considering I just told him I want him to stay away from me for a while, that might be a moot point." When Harrison didn't say anything, Annie raised her eyes to his. "Not going to tell me I'm an idiot?"

Leaning forward on one elbow, her brother said, "Annie, you're one of the smartest people I know. I've seen the good and bad in both you and Kade. Staying away from him is probably a good choice, but I think you owe him the truth about why. Even if he doesn't feel the same way you do, he does care."

"I know he does." She straightened her shoulders. "I intend to tell him. Just not now. Not while he's dealing with so much."

"That makes sense."

She took another sip of her drink. "Am I really one of the smartest people you know?"

He referenced the crowd behind her and joked, "Well, look at your competition."

"Smart-ass." Annie glanced around. The room was full of people she adored and had known forever. None of them were intellectually challenged. Harrison was being unusually sweet. "Have you seen Viviana's brothers today? Didn't you say they were regulars now?"

"They are, but I hear they flew out to Wabonga with a friend of the Barringtons—some guy named Clay. I guess Kade was having issues with his staff and they offered to help him out."

"Really? I can't imagine Kade not handling that himself."

"Like you said, he has a lot going on right now. Besides, when you're suddenly a billionaire, how much could a small local tour company matter to you?"

"Not much, I suppose. Still, he built it up himself."

"The Kade we grew up with is gone, Annie. When the Barringtons leave, you know he's leaving with them."

Annie let out a shaky breath. "Claire said that too."

"I can't imagine it going any other way."

Annie frowned. "Then why the hell do you think I should tell him how I feel?"

He gave her a long hard look. "For you, not for him. Maybe if you say it you'll finally move on."

Maybe.

Annie shook her empty glass at Harrison. "Another round, bartender. Two cherries this time."

Harrison refilled her glass and plopped the maraschino cherries in with dramatic flair. Then his expression turned serious again. "Love sucks."

She cocked her head to one side. Harrison dated, but as far as Annie knew he'd never gotten serious with anyone. "It does. Does she have a name?"

He grinned. "Monday. Tuesday. Wednesday . . ."

Annie laughed and tossed another napkin at him. "You're bad."

He winked. "That's what they say they love about me."

Rolling her eyes, Annie chuckled again. Claire had also been right when she'd said Annie would survive this. *Not just survive . . . I'm determined to thrive again.* She smiled at her brother and resolved to focus on the wonderful people she had in her life rather than the one she didn't.

Chapter Fourteen

TIRED AFTER A sleepless night, Kade forced himself to smile through breakfast at the lodge. He'd gone over what Annie had said again and again but wasn't any closer to understanding what she wanted from him. She needed space because being with him was too hard? Why?

Because they'd had sex?

Because she thought that was all he wanted from her?

She said being with him was hurting her. Well, being without her was slowly killing him.

Around noon, he took Dale and Sophie to his parents' house. Pamela looked nervous when they first arrived, but Sophie spoke to her with such respect and warmth that she relaxed. In much the same way that Dave and Dale had bonded the day before, Sophie and Pamela swapped parenting stories and looked like they respected each other.

Kade was impressed with how comfortable Sophie and Dale seemed in his parents' modest home. They had dressed casually, and if he didn't know how different their lifestyle was, he would have thought the Barringtons could fit into Bright's community perfectly. Sophie loved gardens. Dale loved going out on the water. Kade hadn't known what to expect, but he'd been hopeful after seeing Dave and Dale together.

During a pause in the conversation, Sophie leaned over and spontaneously embraced Pamela. "I'm sorry," she said quickly. "It's just that you're everything I'd hoped you would be."

Stunned, Pamela didn't immediately respond. Her eyes misted. She gave Sophie a brief hug in return. "Thank you. I was nervous about having you here today. Scared, really."

"Oh, my gosh, there's no need to be," Sophie assured her. "You didn't kidnap Kade. You saved him."

"And you gave him as good of a life as we could have. How could we feel anything but love and gratitude toward you?" Dale asked in a thin voice.

Dave put an arm around Pamela's shoulders and rested his chin against her hair. "You did what you had to do, Pam, but you did it out of concern for an innocent. Even I understand that now."

Watching the exchange shifted something inside Kade. He sat forward, elbows on his knees and said, "If it's okay with everyone here, from this day on, I'd like to say I have two dads and two mums. We'll keep it simple and let everyone speculate as they want about the how or why. All that matters is that I think we can make this work."

There wasn't a dry eye in the room, but there was a round of agreement.

Probably to ease the tension of the moment, Dave asked, "So did you hear from that guy Clay who took Dylan and

Connor to Wabonga?"

Kade answered, "I didn't, but Lexi texted me that he contacted her last night. She said he was excited to go into the office today." Still reeling from the emotion of his parents meeting, Clay's plans for the day hadn't been a priority. He probably couldn't do more damage than Kade's drunk, angry office manager had. "I'll call him later."

Dale rubbed his chin. "I can't picture Clay leading an adventure tour."

Kade hadn't bothered to try. "When I gave him directions to my office, I told him all I needed was someone to make a few phone calls. All the information is there. If he wanted to do something wild he could interview one potential hire who has been waiting for me to return. I bet he's bored enough to be back at the lodge by tonight."

"I hear those Sutton boys are a little wild," Dave cautioned. "I have time to go out there to make sure everything is fine."

Although he was fully retired, his father still knew the ins and outs of the business as well as Kade did. Blindfolded, he could do more than Clay and all his cash likely could. "If you have the time and the desire to, that would take a huge weight off me."

Dave clapped a hand on Kade's back. "Are you kidding? I'd love to take the reins back even if it's only for a few days."

Pamela frowned at him. "Don't do anything too strenuous. You know what the doctor said."

Dave stood. "Yes, he said I'm not dead yet."

Kade rose to his feet. Maybe this was a bad idea. "Dad,

all Mum is saying—"

"I have a great idea." Sophie clapped her hands together. "Why don't we make an overnight trip of it? All of us. Dale could do with the fresh air, and I'd love to see Kade's office and operation."

Pamela's smile returned. "Now there's a good idea. By car it's about—"

"We'd fly, Mum. So much easier. I'll look for cheap flights—" He stopped as a realization hit him. "Dale, how hard would it be to get a private plane to take us?"

Dale took out his phone, sent a quick text, then re-pocketed it. "Done."

Kade laughed in surprise. "But we haven't even decided what time we're leaving."

"They'll wait," Dale said as if explaining something everyone knew.

"Where?" Kade asked.

Dale looked to Sophie for guidance. She appeared as lost as he did but supplied slowly, "Anywhere we ask them to?"

It struck Kade then that they genuinely did not understand his confusion. *They* didn't choose their vacations by when hotels and flights were discounted. They didn't wait for people. People waited for them. He didn't know what he felt about entering into that world. What was life like when you removed struggle from it? From the first day he'd met them, he'd sensed he was fundamentally happier than his rich siblings. *Who will I be if I become one of them? Do I even want to be that person?*

"Mum? Dad? You okay with taking a private plane?" he

asked. They both nodded. The Thompsons might be hardworking and grounded, but they weren't fools. Cramped economy airline seat or luxury private plane? No-brainer. "Okay, then. When would you like to leave?"

Just then Kade's phone rang. Connor. *Good, I can tell him they won't need to hold down the fort long.* "G'day, mate. How are you all surviving out there?"

Connor answered in a rush. "Dude, don't be mad, but we lost Clay."

"What do you mean you lost him?" Kade demanded. "In town? Or are you on your way back? Didn't you fly out there together? Don't tell me he decided to drive back alone." The roads through the mountain could be treacherous and Australian high country could be as deadly as it was beautiful.

All four of his parents gathered around. He put Connor on speakerphone.

Connor's next words were likely meant for Dylan. "He's already pissed. I told you we should find Clay before we tell anyone what happened."

"If we knew where he was we wouldn't have to call anyone, would we?" Dylan said sarcastically in the background. There was a scuffling sound like Dylan took the phone. "Listen, it's no one's fault. We decided to take a tour up to the Wabonga Plateau."

"You did what?" Kade roared. "I never okay'd that."

"Chill the fuck out, dude. We were all at your office, bored out of our minds, and a tour showed up but no guide."

"Did you call Todd or any of the names I left? That's what you went there to do."

Connor scoffed, "You have to learn to be more grateful to people who are trying to help you out. None of us went there to be your secretary. And we gave that group a kick-ass tour, so they want to do it again next year. We took a few trucks up the pass. Some of them were hot so I took them skinny-dipping in a waterfall I found."

Holy shit. "Do you know how dangerous that is?"

Dylan interjected, "I took the other half to some cliff and made up the coolest story about how the original settlers of Australia used to throw people off as a sacrifice to the gods. They were all Canadian. I figured they either wouldn't know if it was true or they'd be too nice to call me out on it. I got them real close to the edge and scared the piss out of them. They loved it. Both groups booked for another tour next year. We rocked it."

He didn't want to ask, but he had to. "And Clay?"

Connor groaned. "We're not exactly sure. I thought he was with Dylan. Dylan thought he was with me. I remember him saying he needed to find a toilet. I tried to tell him there wasn't one on a mountain. That might be when we left him. We tried to call him, but none of our phones worked. You really should get a tower up there."

"And nothing from him since?"

"We noticed he wasn't with us when we regrouped at noon," Dylan answered.

"Did you check his hotel room?"

"Of course we—" Dylan stopped, then said, "Connor, go

check his room."

A few minutes later, Connor announced in the background, "He's not there. I had the maid let me in. Nothing. All his stuff looks just like it did this morning." He chuckled. "Oh, and the maid gave me her phone number. She's cute too."

"I need you to tell me exactly where you took those groups." As they did, Kade's stomach twisted painfully. Not only were the roads dangerous in that area, Clay knew nothing about surviving in the bush. Kade looked around at the four adults with him. He'd never been one who liked pranks, but he would have welcomed a glimmer of humor in any of the eyes watching him closely. No, they all looked as concerned as he felt. "Did Clay take anything?"

"I don't know. A backpack maybe? We didn't want to touch your stuff," Dylan said.

That's what they thought I would have minded? "I'm on my way," Kade said tersely. "Don't leave the hotel. I need you near a phone for when I call."

"Okay, you're the boss," Dylan said.

In a more subdued tone, Connor asked, "He's going to be okay, right? All joking aside, we feel really bad."

"He has a much better chance of being okay if we find him while it's daylight. Stay where you are." Kade hung up.

He looked at Dale. "I'm going to need that plane right now."

Dale took out his phone and sent another text. "It's on its way here. Where can it land?"

Kade gave him the name of a small private airfield just

outside of town. He turned to Dave and Pamela. "Mum, can you call the Victoria police? Tell them we have someone lost up there. Call back Connor and Dylan. See if they can remember what Clay was wearing. We want to get feet on the ground and eyes in the air ASAP."

Pamela grabbed a pen and paper and started writing down phone numbers from Kade's phone.

Sophie touched his arm gently. "I'll call the lodge. Everyone will want to help with the search."

In the pause that followed, Dave said, "Kade, call Annie. She's emergency trained. If your friend really is in danger, she has the manpower and the equipment to search the area thoroughly."

Kade accepted his phone back from his mother. Annie had asked him for space, but he hoped she'd take his call. Her fleet was probably booked for the day, but he could compensate her for whatever she might lose. Technically, as a Barrington, if he threw enough money at any helicopter company, they'd probably clear their schedule to help, but there was only one person he wanted at his side.

He dialed her number. "Annie."

She must have heard the urgency in his voice, because in a rush she asked, "What's wrong?"

He quickly brought her up to speed about what Viviana's brothers had told him and the search party he was organizing. Then he waited. He wouldn't have blamed her if she'd said she couldn't do it. She'd already done so much for him.

However, without hesitation she said, "I can have three helicopters at the lodge within the hour. Two more shortly after that. One has to come up from Melbourne, but it might be worth having another set of eyes especially since we're racing against sunset. If I leave now, I can pick you up in fifteen minutes at the field behind the Bartleys'."

"How long should it take to get to Wabonga?" Going with her made more sense than taking a plane if it could get him there sooner.

"An hour or so. Depends on the flight path we can take."

"I'll be in the field." He hung up and let out a harsh breath. "I don't need the private plane, I've got Annie."

Dave nodded in approval. "That sounds about right. We'll take the plane and meet you there."

Kade ran a hand through his hair. "I should have gone back. What the fuck was I thinking?"

"You were taking care of everyone but yourself." Dale put an arm around his wife. "Clay is a grown man. This isn't your fault, Kade."

Fresh from making a phone call, Sophie said, "And you're not alone. If there is one thing Barringtons do well, it's come together in time of crisis. They'll be ready to leave as soon as the choppers arrive. Annie's sending one for us as well. Clay is as good as found."

Pamela walked over and hugged her son. "Kade, you know that mountain. You can do this."

He hugged her back then glanced down at his watch and said, "I'll keep checking my phone. If I don't pick up, call the office. I'll have someone at the phone relaying messages by radio. Dad, take over that job as soon as you get there. I need to go meet Annie."

He walked out of the house, confident that the delegated aspects of the search would be efficiently executed, and waited for the woman he knew would drop everything to help his family. Moments from the past flashed in his mind. He understood now why none of his relationships had progressed beyond dating. Subconsciously he'd planned to return to Annie. It has always been her—always.

A thought came to him that shook him to the core. For her, had it always been him? When he'd left all those years ago, had he hurt her without knowing? Did she have feelings for him she'd never expressed?

Regret tore through him. He'd always tried to do right by people. No, he wasn't perfect, but he had striven to be the good man his father had raised him to be.

Had he failed the only woman he'd ever loved? The thought sickened him.

Funny how chaos could clear a man's head. Stripping his life to the bone had forced him to take stock of not only where he was, but where he wanted to go—and *who* he wanted to go there with. Thompson, Barrington, or somewhere between, he couldn't imagine a version of him that didn't include Annie.

At the sound of her helicopter approaching, Kade squared his shoulders. Now that he knew what he wanted, he felt empowered. Step one: find Clay. Step two: sweep Annie off her feet. Step three: everything else would work out as long as he had Annie at his side.

ANNIE BROUGHT HER helicopter down at a safe distance

from Kade. She didn't make a move to get out or even remove her headset. When it came to search and rescues, every moment mattered. Kade ducked below the blades and climbed into the seat beside her. He clicked on a seat belt, put a headset on, and gave her a thumbs-up. She was back in the air a moment later.

Had Kade called her for coffee, she would have told him again that she needed time to sort herself out. She'd even asked herself if attending Grant and Viviana's wedding was wise. Sure the Barringtons said they wanted her there, but when weighed against how painful it would be to spend more time with Kade, not going made more sense.

She'd considered not picking up when he'd called, but she'd instantly been glad she had. As soon as she'd heard his voice she'd known something was wrong. Everything else had ceased to be a concern in that moment. Broken heart? It could wait. Awkward conversations? They'd return. The safety and welfare of people came first. Personal shit could always be resolved when a crisis was over. That was the way she'd been raised and the only way she wanted to live. Neighbors in Bright might bicker over fences or feud now and then, but when something threatened one of them— they pulled together and overcame it. Life in a mountain town could be harsh and isolating, but people watched out for each other because they had to. That bond was one of the reasons Annie had chosen to not move her base to Melbourne. Yes, she could have found more clients there, but Bright was her home, and even if it made it hard to get over him, Kade would always be part of that.

Over the radio, one of Annie's pilots said, "Approaching the lodge at Lavender Farm now. ETA five minutes. All birds are in the air and on schedule. Contact with family has been made. One or two members will be the eyes for each bird."

Annie glanced at Kade. He looked like he wanted to jump in with a command, but she raised a hand in his direction with a signal for him to hold it. To her pilot she said, "Victoria police have a bird already in the air as well as a medevac fueled up and ready to go. That's the first wave of reconnaissance. Our search areas will be determined by them. Radio me coordinates when you're close."

"Will do," the pilot said.

Kade took out his phone and read over some texts. "Volunteer bushwalkers are being organized and prepped for extended stays. Several four-wheelers and motorcycles have already begun sweeping the roads. I've emergency trained with many of these people for years. Never used them for one of my own, but they're good trackers. My guides are headed into the area also. They might have lost focus when I left, but they take this kind of shit seriously. I'm confident we'll find Clay."

Annie nodded. Kade sounded calm, but she knew him well enough to know that, like her, he could put his emotions on hold to deal with a crisis. Only later would he admit how he actually felt. "Everyone in my fleet is search and rescue trained, and they don't fly without their rescue or med kits. No matter who finds him first, Kade, he'll be in good hands."

There wasn't time for chatter. Annie fielded questions

from her team as well as communicated information back to the volunteers at a base in the foothills of the mountain. Kade also appeared to be in constant communication with a number of people via his phone.

Annie said, "I sent my larger chopper directly to the co-ordination base. It can expedite strategically positioning the bushwalkers. And relocating them if necessary."

Kade put a hand on one of Annie's shoulders. She glanced at him. He said, "You are fucking amazing. Do you know that?"

She smiled. Even though the situation was grave, part-nering with Kade to save someone had been her youthful fantasy of what life would be like for them. Some men might have been threatened by a strong woman, but that had never been Kade. He'd always been genuinely impressed if she beat him in a race. He'd had no desire to get a flying license, said he was much happier climbing a mountain than soaring above it, but he'd celebrated when she'd gotten hers. He'd sat in her passenger seat countless times. Did he have any idea how much that had meant to her? "You're not so bad yourself," she said.

There wasn't time to say much more. Once at the moun-tain, Annie was in constant contact with the local police, coordinating the ground search. Kade had his people check in and take direction from the police as well. There was no room for egos when it came to finding someone lost in the bush. The reality was that even the best team didn't always reach people in time. Australia's high country didn't always give the deceased back, leaving families grieving and searching for decades.

Getting lost in the bush was easy, but survivalists agreed that what happened during the first few hours often determined the outcome. When people became disoriented, they often panicked and made risky decisions. They'd try to cross a dangerous creek, climb down a gorge they otherwise would have avoided. It was unlikely that Clay would head to the higher snow-covered ground, but he could already have been bitten by any number of the poisonous creatures that inhabited Australia's bushland.

Once she and her fleet were flying the designated routes, Annie felt she could finally take a breath. Kade's eyes were glued to the areas they swept over. Without looking away from his task, he said, "Annie, I've only said this about a hundred times this week, but thank you. I know you asked me for time—"

She had. She forced her focus to remain on the path before her as she scanned the ground on her side. She understood. "If the situation were reversed, I would have called you."

"And I would have come. I might not have done everything right, but I hope you know how much you mean to me."

I can't go down that rabbit hole with him now. "I do." She radioed the police that she had swept her section and requested permission to fly over the river. They okay'd it to so she banked in that direction.

"Wait," Kade said. "Annie, Clay isn't a bushwalker. He doesn't even camp. We're searching in the wrong areas. I doubt he studied a map. The cliffs are too steep between where Connor said they saw him last and the river. He won't know where the emergency huts are. We need to think like an inexperienced city person. What would he believe would be the key to his survival?"

Annie could see the logic behind where Kade was going with this. "His phone?"

"Exactly. I bet he's seeking a high point because he thinks he'll get better reception that way."

"He won't, not without a satellite phone."

"We know that, but you've met him, do you think he would?"

"Okay, so all we have to figure out is which high point would look most accessible to him from where he was last seen."

"Pete's Peak." Kade pointed higher up the mountain. "It's on the east side, within walking distance of where Clay was. If he's there, it's thickly forested almost all the way up, but you might be able to land on the clearing at the very top."

"It's worth a shot." Annie radioed in a change of course. "You do know this area well. Do you like it as much as Mount Feathertop?"

"Nothing compares to home," Kade said in a thick voice. "It just took me a long time to realize that. Hopefully not too long."

Rather than read into his words, Annie checked in with her pilots. She also asked the base team if Pete's Peak was known for unusual crosswinds or anything else that would make landing an issue. They gave her an all-clear.

When she landed, Annie cut the engines then retrieved a small pack for Kade. It included a whistle used for communication over distances. He took the pack and slung it over one shoulder. She caught her breath and said, "Kade, be careful."

He gave her a funny look. "I'm not going far."

"There's an emergency beacon in the pack as well. In case anything happens." *Stop.*

"My satellite phone works just fine." He touched her cheek gently.

"Of course."

He leaned closer. "I've taken people to this very spot countless times. There's nothing to worry about."

Annie couldn't have explained her reaction to him considering she hardly understood it herself. She'd prepared herself to survive the idea of not having him in her day-to-day life, but the dire nature of their task had her imagining much worse scenarios. "Check in ever fifteen minutes or so for my sanity."

A crooked grin stretched his lips. "You do care." He placed his hands on her hips and pulled her flush against him.

She put her hands on his powerful chest but didn't push him away. "Don't."

He looked into her eyes with such intensity that Annie nearly lost her ability to breathe. Her eyes fluttered shut when his lips brushed over hers. What had started innocent enough, quickly deepened. It overtook both of them, leaving them shuddering when they parted. "I'm sorry. I have to go, Annie," he said huskily.

She nodded wordlessly.

He shook his head as if to clear it. "There are things that need to be said, but—"

"Go," she said softly. "I'll be right here waiting for you."

A frown creased his forehead, and he gave her one passionate kiss then stepped away without saying more. She watched him walk down a steep hill before disappearing into a wooded area. He alternated calling out Clay's name with whistle blows.

Annie went to her radio to call in an update on their location. "I'm waiting with the helicopter." She replaced the radio.

She stood there, fingers pressed to her lips, wondering where the hell she and Kade were headed. Toward one last friend fuck?

No, I won't make that mistake again.

Come on, Clay, be where Kade thinks you are.

I need to get home, concentrate on myself for a while, and start over. Not angry. Not sad. Just stronger and wiser.

Chapter Fifteen

KADE BLEW THE whistle one time then waited for any type of response. Clay probably wouldn't know the code behind the number of sounds, but any other searchers who might be in earshot would. One was a question: Where are you?

Although he hadn't yet found Clay, Kade had found answers in Annie's kiss. She wasn't breaking it off with him because she wasn't interested. She wasn't angry with him. She'd told him being with him was hurting her, and he felt that conflict in her.

Because she doesn't know how I feel about her. How could she when I just figured it out myself?

She will, though. As soon as this is over, she will.

In the distance, a whistle blew in response.

Kade froze and blew his whistle again.

Once again there was an answering blast. Kade headed in the direction of it. He repeated the call and followed the response until he spotted the outline of a tall man coming toward him. Clay looked sweaty and his legs were scratched, but he was walking fine and his color was good.

"G'day mate," Clay said in a poor impression of an Australian accent. "You're a welcome sight."

"You hurt at all?" Kade asked.

Clay shook his head. "No, but I've discovered I'm not into nature. Or hiking. Or bugs." He shuddered. "There's also a sad lack of public facilities out here."

Kade took out his phone to tell Annie he'd found Clay.

"Oh, thank God," she said. "How is he?"

After looking him over again, Kade announced, "Not hurt. Other than that, about how you'd guess."

"I'll radio down that we found him, and inform my crew as well. Do you want me to contact your parents?"

"Please. We'll be back with you in ten to twenty."

"Sounds good. See you then."

Kade turned and started walking, leaving Clay to trot after him. The sooner this was over the sooner he could repair things with Annie.

Clay said, "Hey, where are you going?"

"Back to the helicopter. You might want to follow me." He wouldn't normally be so abrupt with someone who had just gone through a traumatic experience. Clay didn't look worse for wear, though. In fact, there was a cockiness to him that was striking a nerve.

"Well, aren't we testy," Clay said with some humor.

"That's it." Kade stopped and spun on his heel. "You need to shut the hell up. People die in these mountains. If your arse had, it would have been nothing more than you deserve, but you and Viviana's brothers led a group of innocent people up here under the false pretense that any of you knew what the fuck you were doing. That's what is going up my arse the most. It's not just your life you don't care about. Had something happened to those people, you wouldn't even have been able to contact someone for help."

Raising both hands in surrender, Clay said, "Calm down, did something happen? Everyone else made it back, right?"

"Yes, but no thanks to you." Advancing on him, Kade growled, "At least look like you fucking care. There are about a hundred people who dropped everything and put their lives at risk to find you. Most of them are volunteers. Some won't get paid for today because instead of reporting to their jobs, they wasted their time searching for an idiot who had no business being here at all. I made it clear that all you were supposed to do was run damage control in my office."

Clay's expression lost all humor. When he answered it was in a quiet tone. "I clearly didn't think this through."

Kade ran a hand through his hair and sighed. "All I'm saying is this isn't a joke to anyone. When you meet the rescue team, and you will because they'll be with the emergency team who will want to see you before you leave—don't be a dick."

Clay nodded once then followed Kade silently back to the peak. Annie met them where the trees opened up.

She gave Clay an assessing once-over then turned her attention to Kade. "It was a good idea to try the peak, Kade."

Kade caressed the line of her jaw with a brush of his fingertips. God, he could hardly wait to kiss his way from her ear to every other inch of her. "Sometimes I know what I'm doing."

Her face flushed and she stepped back, breaking the contact between them. "The police want to speak to Clay before he leaves. They asked us to meet them in a field at the entrance of Kimball Road. I figured you'd know where that is."

"I do. That's old man Kimball's field. He and his wife open their property and their home once a month to the Victoria Search and Rescue volunteers for training purposes. It's a tradition that started because the farm is conveniently located, and Kimball was one of the founding volunteers, but we all joke that it remains an integral part of the training program because his wife makes the best chicken parmi and pav." Kade wanted that kind of future with Annie. Something solid that would also bring some good into the world. He had no idea what that would look like for them, but the more he thought about it the more certain he was that it was the path they were meant to take.

As if she could sense his thoughts, she flushed again and looked away. "Well, the sooner we get over there the sooner we can all go home."

Home sounded pretty damn good to Kade.

Clay stepped forward. Thankfully he'd left his smug humor back in the bush. "Annie, thank you for coming to find me."

Kade met the man's gaze. "She didn't come by herself. Every client on her schedule had to find an alternative means of transportation. She called back all her pilots to fly the Barringtons out here to assist in the search. Some are here, some are still en route."

"Holy shit. I wasn't lost that long," Clay said, going a little pale.

"Like I said, not everyone who gets lost in these mountains survives the experience."

"Well," Clay said, "I really appreciate it."

"I'm just glad you're okay." Annie gave Clay a sympathetic look. "You're one of the lucky ones. This is the outcome we all pray for." She opened the back door of the helicopter. Clay climbed in.

Kade stepped between Annie and the pilot door. "Today reminds me of that day you flew with the firefighters. I was proud of you then. I'm proud of you now."

She smiled. "Thank you. You should be proud of yourself as well. Your instincts were spot-on."

He took her hand in his. "We make a good team."

A storm raged in her eyes, and she slid her hand out of his. "I don't mean to be rude, but I need to get back. I have some disgruntled clients to appease. My competition very happily took over the runs. You know how that can go."

"What do you need?" Kade asked. "Say it and it's yours. I'm sure with my new connections I can easily get you enough new clients you won't even miss the ones you lost. Hell, as a thank you I could double the size of your fleet. I'm sure I can afford it now."

"I'll be fine, Kade." She stepped past him, climbed into the pilot seat, and closed her door in his face.

He rushed around to the other side of the helicopter. She didn't spare him so much as a glance as she started the engine up and took off. He hadn't meant to offend her, but she definitely didn't look happy with him.

Through his headset radio, Clay asked, "Has anyone spoken to Lexi? How angry is she?"

As soon as they landed, Annie, Kade, and Clay were separated. Clay was taken to be examined by the medical team while an officer asked him questions. Kade was warmly welcomed by the local volunteers, as well as one very apologetic-looking man Annie guessed was the one who had originally been left in charge of Kade's office.

Annie had just finished debriefing with one of the officers when her pilots began to land, delivering a good number of the Barrington family. She gasped when the door of one helicopter flew open mere seconds after it landed and didn't breathe properly until the woman cleared the rotors. *That would have been a bloody mess. Literally.*

Annie brought a shaking hand to her mouth. She was tired and her nerves were shot. As vulnerable as she was, she knew she had to escape before Kade felt compelled to thank her again. She didn't want his gratitude any more than she wanted to be paid off. He was already changing—already becoming a Barrington. It was only a matter of time before his opinion of Bright along with his simple life there changed.

He really is leaving even if he doesn't see it yet.

Annie sought out one of her pilots to tell her she was leaving. "Mel, can you handle organizing everyone on this side? The family will all need to get home. Tell everyone to log their hours, and I'll compensate them with overtime pay."

"Will do," her longtime pilot said. Mel had grown up in Bright and had been a stay-at-home mum until her children had started school. Annie had funded flight school for her, and the payoff had been a reliable and loyal second-in-command who was also a damn good pilot. She referenced the elated group. "Are you sure you want to miss out on all that? You're the one who found him."

Annie shrugged. "Not really. I didn't do anything more than anyone else here. We were just lucky he was where Kade thought he might be."

Mel had known her long enough to ask, "Is Kade flying back with you?"

Annie squared her shoulders. "No."

"I'm sorry," Mel said, hugging Annie.

Annie almost told her it was no big deal, but she simply hugged her back instead. Mel was a friend as well as an employee. There was no reason to hide the truth from her.

"Annie?" Lexi's voice interrupted.

Annie looked up from hugging Mel to see Lexi and Clay standing there. Mel excused herself and slipped away. "Yes?"

Lexi wrapped her arms around Annie and hugged her tightly. Clay joined in. Laughing when they finally released her, Annie said, "You're welcome."

Looking more serious than Annie had ever seen him, Clay said, "I feel bad, and I'm not used to feeling this way. What can I do for you as a token of appreciation? Something that says thank you for saving my sorry ass?"

Tucking herself beneath one of Clay's arms, Lexi said,

"I've never been so scared. Seriously, what can we do to show you how grateful we are?"

Annie looked at the volunteers still gathered and said, "I'm fortunate to be in a place where I don't need anything, but not everyone here is so lucky. First, fund Wabonga's search and rescue team. Cover what it cost them to look for you today. Then, if you want to express your gratitude, do something good for this community. Every single person who geared up to find you is a hero, and it would be nice to see them recognized for it."

Lexi and Clay exchanged a look then nodded. Clay asked, "But you don't want anything for yourself? Why do I get the feeling you're going to fly off as soon as we walk away?"

Lexi gushed, "We're all heading back to the lodge after this. You have to come with."

Annie shook her head. "It has been a long and crazy day, but it's not over for me yet. I have work waiting for me back at my office."

"I'm sure—" Clay started to say then stopped and glanced over to where Kade was talking to the police officer. When his gaze returned to Annie, he said, "Lexi and I will definitely take your advice and make sure good things happen for this town and these people in particular."

Annie smiled.

Clay continued, "But we will do something for you. When the time comes, just accept it."

Lexi cocked her head to one side. "What are you thinking, Clay?"

He looked at Lexi. "I say we organize the biggest, most kick-ass wedding Australia has ever seen for her and Kade."

His offer hit Annie like a sucker punch to the gut. She swayed on her feet. "That's an incredibly generous offer, but sadly it won't be necessary."

Fighting a sudden burst of panic, Annie bolted to her helicopter and took off before anyone else had a chance to make her feel worse than she already did. Back at her office, she forced herself to connect with each and every client who had been affected that day. She didn't pick up when Kade called. She didn't respond to his text. Instead she contacted her competition to thank them for their cooperation.

Kade was a grown man who could take care of himself.

His family was safely all together again.

It was time for Annie to put her needs first. She put her feet up on her desk, leaned back in her chair, and called Claire. A true friend, Claire hardly said a word as the details of the day spilled out of Annie. "So, I left," Annie concluded. "It was the only choice that made sense. I'm going to do what you and I agreed would be best for me. I'm going to give myself some time away from him. At least for now, I won't answer his phone calls or his texts. It's over."

"Is it?" Claire asked slowly.

Wow, she doesn't have much faith in me, does she? "I'm serious. You were right. Kade doesn't need me. We have a chemistry right now that's tempting, but giving in to it will only get me hurt again. I'm glad I was able to be there for him, now I need to do what's best for me." When Claire didn't instantly confirm that it was the right choice, Annie asked, "What are you not saying?"

Claire let out an audible breath. "You've stumped me on this one. I don't know what I think about you and Kade anymore."

"There is no me and Kade," Annie said with a frown. "That's what I have finally come to peace with."

"Okay."

"I have."

"If you say so."

"We're done. You won't even hear his name after today."

Claire made a sympathetic sound. "I love you, Annie. Be kind to yourself."

"I will. Bye. I'll talk to you tomorrow about work and things that are important enough to mention."

"Night, Annie."

"Night, Claire."

Chapter Sixteen

IMMEDIATELY AFTER SPEAKING to the police officer, Kade turned to look for Annie but was intercepted by his brother Andrew and his wife, Helene.

"Do you have a minute?" Andrew asked gruffly.

Not feeling like he had much of a choice, Kade looked around the area one more time. He'd heard a helicopter take off earlier, but he hadn't for a moment thought it might have been hers. He didn't see it, though, nor her. Shit.

Holding on to Andrew's arm, Helene said, "Just say it, Andrew."

Andrew cleared his throat and the pained expression on his face was enough to put a brake on Kade's need to chase Annie. Fifteen minutes more or less wouldn't change the outcome of the conversation Kade intended to have with Annie.

After wiping a hand over his face, Andrew said, "I told myself there would be time later to tell you everything, but when I heard Clay was missing I realized that few things happen on the timetable we'd choose. I don't mean to dump this on you right now, but I have to get it off my chest."

"Okay." Kade had an idea what he was about to say, but not the details. His guess was that Helene or her family were somehow involved in his disappearance.

Andrew put an arm around Helene and kissed her forehead before saying, "This woman is an angel who brought me back from hell. She's completely innocent in all this."

Helene placed her hand on Andrew's chest. "Kade, my uncle owned the clinic you were taken from. When people started dying, he took a bribe to cover it up. There's no excuse for what he did, and I'm the only reason he hasn't paid for that crime. When Andrew came to Aruba looking for clues about what had happened to you, he met me."

Face tight, Andrew said, "I didn't expect to find clues or love. I didn't honestly believe you were still alive and none of us wanted another ugly truth to face. Helene had no idea what her uncle had done before we uncovered his secret together."

With tears in her eyes, Helene hugged Andrew's side. "Andrew would have told you right away, but he wanted to protect me. I don't need to be protected. I need to know I'm not what stands between the two of you being the brothers you were born to be."

"Helene—" Andrew started to say.

"It's okay," Kade said, interrupting whatever Andrew had been about to say. "Helene, you have nothing to worry about from me. I have a good life here. I'm not angry. I don't feel cheated. I'll admit it took a while to get used to the idea of all of you, but now that I have, this experience has been good for me. I see things more clearly. I'm more grateful for my life here. That probably doesn't make any sense, but although I am haunted by how many lives were negatively affected by my abduction, it's impossible for me to imagine not having been raised here with all the people who have been brought into my life. We're good, Andrew. All of us."

Andrew held out his hand for Kade to shake.

Following an impulse, Kade gave him a back-thumping hug instead that put a smile on Helene's face. She hugged Kade next.

With a cautious smile, Andrew said, "That went a lot easier than I thought it would."

Seeking to lighten the mood, Kade added, "I could say the same about finding Clay."

Andrew whistled. "When those helicopters started landing on the lawn of the lodge, it was like the cavalry had arrived." He put his arm around Helene's waist again. "If you're lucky enough to meet a woman who has your back like that, you don't let her get away."

Helene touched Andrew's cheek gently. "Something tells me he won't. You Barrington men are pretty smart when it comes to that."

Kade pocketed his hands and sighed. "I don't know if I'd call myself smart. It took Annie telling me she didn't want to see me anymore for me to realize that I'm in love with her."

"I could have told you that the first time I saw the two of you together," Andrew said with a grin.

Helene elbowed Andrew playfully. "Don't tease him." After glancing around, Helene asked, "Is she still here?"

Kade shook his head.

"That's actually a good thing," Andrew claimed.

Kade's eyebrows shot up in doubt. "How so?"

"It gives you time to plan your countermeasure."

Nodding in agreement, Helene added, "The perfect proposal."

"A proposal." They were an optimistic bunch, those Barringtons. "Should I lead with that considering she's not speaking to me right now?"

"In nature," Helene said with conviction, "it's never the timid who win the mate."

Andrew chuckled. "She tends to explain human behavior in terms of animals. You get used to it."

"Hey," Helene protested. "Humans are mammals. We think we've evolved beyond the other creatures who inhabit the planet with us, but make us the least bit uncomfortable or unsure and watch how primal people get."

"Although I appreciate this talk, I can handle it from here on my own."

Connor and Dylan appeared beside Andrew before Kade had a chance to make his escape. Dylan punched Kade in the arm. "Good job today. I'm so glad Clay's not dead."

Connor nodded in agreement. "That would have been bad. It's okay, though. Clay accepted our apology. He actually got a little emotional over it."

Dylan grunted. "You were hugging him so tight you made his eyes water."

Connor shrugged. "He was touched by my sincerity."

Dylan rolled his eyes. "He was touched all right. You lifted him right off his feet. You don't do that to another dude, Connor."

"I'll hug whoever I want. If you don't stop, I'll pick your ass up right now and squeeze you like a toothpaste tube until you cry for Dad." Connor made a grab for Dylan.

Viviana and Grant joined the group. Viviana said, "Kade, I hope my brothers said what they intended to when they came over."

Both Connor and Dylan froze and turned to Kade. Dylan was the first to speak. "Sorry we didn't ask you if we could lead one of your tours."

Obediently, as if he were reciting something he'd been told to say, Connor added, "We didn't think it through, and someone could have been seriously injured. Next time we'll ask you first."

Grant grimaced. "I tried to explain to them there won't be a next time."

Connor's jaw dropped in shock. "Of course there will be. Dude, those Canadians are coming back just to see this glorious body naked again." He struck a bodybuilding pose. "You can't disappoint them."

It might have been the sheer absurdity of them, but Kade couldn't give the same lecture to Viviana's brothers that he gave to Clay. And, really, what was the likelihood they'd be in Australia the following year anyway? "I'm sure we can figure something out."

"I knew it," Dylan said, his chest puffing up with pride. "Now that Clay is back, I think you'll see your business needs someone like us. I mean, we have to go home eventually because Dad needs us, but we won't leave you in a bind,

Kade."

"Thanks, mate," Kade said, hoping his amusement wasn't obvious. "I'm going to temporarily close the doors of the tour company, at least until I figure a few other things out."

Grant leaned in. "If you need something, Kade . . ."

"No. I'm good, Grant. I may reopen or I may not. I thought the business was what was important, but it was the reason behind it that mattered. I can take care of my parents now without being so far away from them." He looked around at who had come when he needed them. Mum and Dad were standing with Sophie and Dale. All of his siblings were there. This was his family, and it finally felt right to call them that. There was one important person missing, though. Getting her back was his new priority.

"Viviana, do you have a moment?" Kade motioned for his future sister-in-law to step aside with him. She linked arms with him as they walked. "I don't know how best to move forward with Annie. On one hand, I finally know what I want. I'm still figuring out the whole Kade/Kent thing. I'm sure that will take me to Boston for a while, and I want her with me. On the other hand, she said she wants time away from me, which I respect. I respect her. How do I show her I love her if she doesn't want to talk to me? The last thing I want is to hurt her again."

Viviana placed a hand over her rounded stomach. "You're a good guy, Kade/Kent Thompson/Barrington. I don't know Annie well enough to understand why she pulled away, but there's one person who definitely does."

"Annie."

"You got it," Viviana said with a smile. "Women are complicated, but there's only two reasons they usually tell a man to stay away. Either because they're not interested, or because they're afraid of being hurt. From everything I've seen, I don't believe for a second that Annie isn't in love with you. So, ask yourself . . . what would she fear you'll do again?"

"Leave." It made sense. They'd never fought. He'd never betrayed her or even lied to her. "She's afraid when everything settles I'm going to leave without her. That has to be it."

Viviana nodded. "So what are you going to do?"

Squaring his shoulders, he said, "I'm going to show her I'm not going anywhere this time."

With a smile of approval, Viviana said, "Grant bought me a house and moved his office to my hometown. That's what convinced me he was serious."

"Damn," Kade said with humor. "I've got to up my game."

Chapter Seventeen

ANNIE WAS IN her office early the next morning going over the next week's flight schedule for her pilots. A bouquet of purple hydrangea killed her ability to concentrate, especially the card tucked into the flowers.

She took it to her desk without opening it. Moving forward would mean breaking old patterns. Believing, even for a second, that the flowers were from Kade would send her up and down the roller coaster of emotion she'd sent herself on too many times in the past.

The most likely sender was Clay as a thank-you for finding him. Sophie or Dale might have sent them to show their appreciation for transporting the Barringtons to Wabonga. Either way, there was no way they were from Kade.

Which was for the best.

Flowers from Kade would have been in lieu of an apology, and she didn't need another one of those from him. He had nothing to be sorry for. *The only issue we have—the only one we've ever had—is because I'm an idiot.*

No, not an idiot . . . just a woman who has feelings for a man who has never returned them. That doesn't make me stupid, it makes me human.

I can't change the past, but I can strive to do better.

She stood up and stretched, sore from running on her treadmill the night before and once again in the morning.

Annie had come up with a plan the night before as she'd lain awake wondering if Kade had gotten home safely and how he was getting on with his family. She decided every time she was tempted to call Claire about Kade, or worse, call Kade, she'd exercise instead. So, at two a.m. when her mind had refused to turn off and let her sleep, she ran on her treadmill. When she'd woken up at the crack of dawn and been tempted to see if Kade had texted her again, she ran for another thirty minutes.

Looks like I'll be investing in a treadmill for my office as well.

Her phone rang. *Claire.* "Hey, you," Annie said in a forced cheerful voice.

"How's your morning going?"

Not going to mention him. Nope, not doing it. "Same ole, same ole. I had one of my pilots call in sick so I'm juggling schedules. How's your day so far?"

"Just the usual for me as well. You know the new Courtney movie that's releasing this summer? The thriller? They're doing some filming in Melbourne. I passed your info along to the production company in case they need transport anywhere."

"You rock, Claire. Did you ever hear from that woman I gave your card to? The one who was nervous about taking over her family's business?"

"Elizabeth. Yes. I adore her. All she needed was validation that she knew what to do." There was a pause, then Claire asked, "So, seriously, nothing new or unusual today?"

Annie glanced at the flowers. Had Claire sent them? Is she waiting for me to thank her? "I did get flowers, but I haven't had time to open the card yet."

"Seriously?"

"Okay, I decided to not open it until after work."

"Wow, that's real willpower."

"Don't congratulate me yet, they arrived about fifteen minutes ago. Are they from you?"

"No."

Interesting. "But you knew they were coming?"

"Yes."

"Are they from the Barringtons?"

"In a way."

Annie threw a hand up in the air in exasperation. "Oh, for God's sake, just tell me who sent them."

"It came with a card, Annie."

Annie grabbed the card from her desk but hesitated before opening it. "If it's from him it doesn't matter. I know he cares about me. I know he doesn't want to see me hurt. Hopefully, soon, I'll be in a place where I can see a bouquet of flowers from him and not want to throw them back in his face. I don't want to be angry with him. I don't want to be disappointed in myself. You're right. I was fine without him. I'll be fine again. I'm just not there yet."

"Open the card."

What the fuck? Annie tore the card open.

Call me. —Kade

She read it aloud to Claire. "Well, that says nothing I didn't already know."

"Oh," Claire said, "he told me it would explain how he feels."

"It does. He feels like I should call him. Hey, since when do you and Kade talk?"

"Since Harrison gave him my number last night."

"Why would Harrison do that?"

"Because like me, your brother wants this to work out for the two of you."

"Wait, work out, like become good friends again? Maybe someday. We talked about this, Claire. You're the one who told me to cut the cord."

"He loves you, Annie."

"No," Annie said emphatically, her tone rising with her emotions. "Don't do this. I can't go back there. You of all people should understand why I can't."

"At least answer his texts. Give him one more chance."

"No. One more chance? That's exactly what I swore I'd stop doing. It's not healthy. He's an addiction, remember? You said all that. I don't understand your about-face."

"I had a long talk with him last night, Annie. He has so much he wants to tell you."

Annie sat at her desk and covered her face with one hand. "I can't do it, Claire. I can't go to him, hoping he'll say what I've always wanted him to, believing he might, and risking he won't. A piece of me dies every time I do. No. I'm not putting myself through that again." A horrifying thought came to Annie. "Claire, you didn't tell him how I feel about him, did you?"

Of all the worst-case scenarios Annie could think of, having Kade say he loved her simply because he felt sorry for her was at the top of the list. If Kade felt guilty about sleeping with her, he might feel he needed to say something to make her feel better.

"No. Never. I'd never do that to you."

"Then why now? Why would Kade say he loves me *now*?"

"How about because he turned to you in a time of need and you were there for him the way you always have been?" Her tone turned wry. "The sex probably helped him along as well."

Flashes from the night they'd shared came back to Annie, bringing warmth to her cheeks. It had been the best she'd ever had, but had it been the same for him? "I'm not doing this, Claire. I'm not calling him."

"Okay."

"I've got a shitload of work on my desk and a new client who wants a round trip to Melbourne later today. Even if I wanted to call him, I don't have time."

"I understand."

"Kade's confused right now. That makes sense. His whole life is upside down. But what about a week from now? A month? Even if he thinks he feels something for me today, what will happen a year from now when he's not overwhelmed anymore?"

Claire sighed. "I'll support whatever you decide, Annie,

but I've never held back my honest opinion. This time seems different." A bell sounded in the background. "I have to go, my next client just walked in. Call me if you need me."

"I will." Before she hung up, Annie added, "And thank you for caring enough to want to help."

"Always, babe. Always."

Claire hung up and Annie sat, staring at her phone. She drummed her fingers on either side of it. Stood up. Sat back down. Drummed her fingers again.

KADE DIDN'T SIT idly by waiting for Annie to call him. He asked Sophie, Dale, Pamela, Dave, Mitch, and Hazel to meet him at the pub before it opened for lunch. Harrison had arranged for a light breakfast to be served.

Once they were all seated and sipping coffee at a round table in the dining area, Kade rose to his feet and cleared his throat. "I'm sure you're all wondering why I gathered you this morning."

"Isn't it just for us to meet?" Hazel asked.

"That was part of it." Kade looked around at the three couples who'd each played a significant role in his life. "When I ask myself what kind of father—what kind of parent—I want to be, all I need to do is look around at the examples each of you have been for me. Mum and Dad, you took me in and raised me as your own. I never knew a day without your love and support. Sophie and Dale, you never let loss or anger beat you. You held your family together and came out the other side stronger. Hazel and Mitch, I never remember a time when I felt unwelcome in your home. Your love didn't stop at your biological children, and I'm a better person because of it."

Mitch looked around the table anxiously. "He's not dying, is he?"

Dave answered, "Not as of yesterday, but Kade why don't you say what you brought us here for? Not all of us have the healthy hearts we used to."

Here goes. "I'm going to ask Annie to marry me, and I'd like your blessing . . . all of your blessings." Kade held his breath and waited.

"It's about damn time," Hazel said.

Mitch nodded in agreement. "You sure did drag your feet on that one, Kade."

Pamela laughed. "Who hasn't seen that one coming since high school?"

Dave frowned. "Didn't you say she's not taking your calls?"

With a huge smile, Sophie hugged her husband. "Dale, we have so much to celebrate. I never thought we'd be this happy again, but look at us."

Dale gave his wife's arm a pat and her temple a kiss. "There certainly is a lot to be happy about." He turned his gaze to Kade. "Now, what is this about her not taking your calls? We just saw her yesterday." He looked at Mitch. "You raised an amazing daughter. We have so much to thank her for already."

"She's pretty great," Mitch agreed then turned to Kade. "And she isn't quick to anger. What did you do?"

Kade took his seat and sighed. "It's what I didn't do. I

didn't realize what we had until I came home and saw her again, and even then I was thick about it. Annie's always been important to me. You know that. I've always loved her, but it's different now. I'm also in love with her. I've spent the last week trying to figure out who I am, and what I realized is my name doesn't matter. I don't care about money beyond being able to pay my bills. My family and friends matter to me. I can't imagine my life without everyone at this table—or without Annie. She asked me to give her time, so I'm respecting that, but I intend to have everything in place for when she calls."

Seated beside him, Sophie fidgeted with a green, shield-shaped diamond on her left hand while looking at her husband. Then she slid the ring off. "Kade, Dale gave this to me for our thirtieth anniversary. It took us a long time to get back to a good place, but we finally did and this was a representation of the good in our lives. If you don't already have one and if it looks like a ring Annie would like, we'd be honored if you gave it to her when you propose."

Kade accepted the ring. Ten years of his old income probably couldn't have purchased it. Would Annie like it? She wasn't into material things, but he was certain that once she knew where it came from she would be moved by Sophie's thoughtfulness, just as he was. He leaned over and gave her a kiss on the cheek. "Thank you, Mum. It's perfect."

Tears filled Sophie's eyes even as she smiled.

Kade glanced at Pamela and she had a similar expression on her face as she wiped tears from the corners of her eyes.

Leaning forward, Hazel said, "I couldn't ask for a better son-in-law." She winked. "But I kind of hope she makes you work for it."

"I'm sure she will." Kade chuckled.

His phone rang. He almost ignored it, taught by several seated there to not use a phone at the table. There was a chance, though, just a chance that it could be Annie so he whipped out his phone.

And accidentally dropped it to the floor when her name showed on the caller ID.

"It's her," he said in a rush, bending to retrieve his phone.

"Don't mind us," Pamela joked. "We'll just be sitting here on the edge of our seats hanging on your every word."

Dave shook his head with a smile. "Step away and talk to her, Son. We'll all be here when you're done."

As he walked away from the table, he heard Hazel say, "Don't mess this up. Tell her how you feel."

"He'll do fine," Pamela assured her, then added, "I hope."

"I'm sure he can handle this," Sophie interjected.

An insulting amount of groaning followed her comment. Kade called back to them, "Have a little faith."

He swiped to answer her call just in time to miss it.

Fuck.

Chapter Eighteen

ANNIE DROPPED HER phone to her desk, hating herself for calling him, hating him for not answering. It was a roller-coaster ride she knew well—one that ended with an abrupt crash into reality. *Why do I do this to myself? Why don't I ever learn?*

Her phone began to light up with a call from Kade she was no longer prepared for. She let it ring through to her messages, choosing to walk out of her office into the hangar attached to it. She'd purchased the land and built all this. She'd done it on her own. No man needed.

She stepped outside into the sunshine and tipped her face back, letting the warmth of it wash over her. A walk around her property made her feel a little better. No one else had the power to make her doubt herself. She was a strong, independent woman.

Plagued by a fantasy it was time to let go of.

Her father loved to tell how he'd known Hazel was the woman for him from the very first time he'd laid eyes on her. *I've heard that story my whole life, which is why I believed in that kind of love.*

I don't know if it was my fault, my lack of courage when it came to telling him how I felt, but it didn't turn out that way for me, Dad. And I'm losing faith in love altogether.

She headed inside toward her first helicopter. She'd kept it as a reminder of the humble beginnings of her journey. As she ran her hand over a patch of rust on its door, she admitted she'd also kept it because it was what she'd flown with Kade. Letting go had so many layers.

"You finally gonna let me fix your baby up?" Will, her full-time mechanic, asked. Bald and about Annie's height, but strong like a bulldog, he was an integral part of her organization. His wife joked that his excitement over working on a brand-new helicopter was rivaled only by the births of their three children.

With her hand still resting on the helicopter's door, Annie said, "I'm thinking about finally scrapping her."

"No."

Annie dropped her hand. "She doesn't do anything but take up space and make visiting clients worry we might send her to pick them up. It's time to let her go and focus on where the company is headed rather than where it came from."

Will pulled a cloth from his pocket and used it to polish the nose of the helicopter. "Do what you want, but to me she's the heart of this place."

"She doesn't deserve that status. There's a reason we don't fly her anymore. Why hold on to something that won't ever be what I need?"

Will scratched the back of his neck and gave her a long

look. "Everyone is still buzzing about Kade's rich relatives and your mountain rescue. Your mood doesn't have anything to do with that, does it?"

Annie frowned and folded her arms across her chest. "My mood?"

Will grinned. "Now, don't go looking at me like my wife does when I stay for an extra beer with my mates. You haven't been yourself since Kade came back to town. We can dance around it and pretend you're fine, but we all know how you feel about him."

Fisting her hands, Annie declared, "This isn't about Kade. Not everything in my life is. I helped him when he needed help. So what? It wasn't more than I would have done for anyone else. A week from now he'll by flying off with his American family. Do you think he'll give any of us a second thought? He won't. So, no, I'm not wasting my time feeling anything for him."

"You don't mean that, Annie," Kade said from behind her. "And I'm not going anywhere—not without you."

Annie jumped and spun around to face him.

"G'day, Kade." Will shook his hand then motioned toward the office. "I'm gonna see if I can get Annie's flights for today covered."

"Don't you dare, Will," Annie ground out.

Will froze.

Kade held her gaze. "You know we need to talk, Annie."

Annie planted her feet and raised her chin. "I don't want to do this, Kade. I can't be what you use to make yourself feel better."

Kade stepped closer. "That's not what you are to me."

"I'm just going to go—" Will began.

"Stay, Will," Annie ordered. "This won't take long, and then we have a lot of work to do." She swallowed hard and plowed forward. "Kade, being confused is natural, considering everything going on in your life. You may think you have feelings for me right now, but they weren't there before everything came crashing down, and I don't believe they'll be there when the dust settles. You should focus on yourself right now and getting to know your family."

Kade stepped closer still. "I'm not confused. I know exactly what I want."

It was always difficult to concentrate when he was close. Annie took a deep breath and held her ground. What she wanted to do was throw her arms around his neck and kiss him while praying he'd say those three words she'd waited so long to hear from him, but she didn't. She refused to be that woman ever again. "Goodbye, Kade."

Will groaned. "Kade, sounds like you should go."

"I love you, Annie," Kade said huskily. "I'm sorry it took me so long to see it."

Tears blurred Annie's vision. She shook her head as she stepped back. "You think you do, but you'll thank me one day for not believing you." With that she spun, ran back to her office, and slammed the door behind her.

KADE AND WILL stood in the hangar watching her go. Kade broke the awkward silence that followed the slam of her door. "That didn't go quite the way I'd hoped."

Will rocked back on his heels and shrugged. "Women are tough."

Which led to a natural question of, "How's the family? Marion and the kids?"

"Good. My youngest is getting ready for uni. Can you believe it? I can't. I'm not getting any older so how are they?"

Kade sighed. Time did have a way of getting away from a person. He'd never intended to be away as long as he had. He'd still be gone if the Barringtons hadn't shown up in Bright. No wonder Annie didn't believe him. He'd done nothing to prove her fears wrong.

Absently he looked around the hangar as if there might be something there that could remedy the situation. He instantly recognized Annie's first helicopter. Back in high school she'd scraped money together and bought it even though no one in her family knew a thing about flying. He remembered watching her take it up for the first time with her instructor as vividly as he remembered his own first flight in it. It had never been pretty, but mechanically it had been a good choice. She'd loved it so much she'd named it.

Shit. How could he have forgotten the name? He ran a hand over the side of the two-seater helicopter.

"She's getting rid of it," Will said from beside him.

His head snapped back. "Why? She loves it."

"Said it's time to move on."

Kade's gut clenched painfully. "No, she didn't hold on to it for this long to let go of it now." *She can't love me this long to give up just when I figured out she's my future—my forever.*

"Forever," Kade said aloud. "That's what she called it because she thought it would take her forever to pay it off."

He slapped the door of the little helicopter. "She'd intended to restore it. Paint. New seats. Polish it up."

"Never made sense to put her money into that. She made the practical choice of investing in newer aircrafts."

"I want to do it for her, Will. Will you help me make that happen?"

Will didn't answer at first. He looked from the closed office door to the helicopter and back to Kade. "Listen, that woman is one of the kindest, most loyal people I've ever known. I'm damn lucky to work for her. None of us want to see her hurt. If you're not sure where your heart is at, leave. No harm, no foul. But if you do this, you'd better have a fucking ring in mind."

Kade dug into the pocket of his jeans and pulled out the huge green diamond Sophie had given him a short while earlier. "Like this one?"

With a toothy grin and a clap on the back, Will said, "Strewth. Exactly the fuck like that. Okay. Let's do this."

Kade and Will exchanged phone numbers. "I'll send someone to pick it up. I'd like to give it back to her this weekend."

Will whistled. "That fast? Forever needs a lot of work. I don't see it happening."

"You just concentrate on helping me get it out of here without her knowing I'm the one who took it. I'll handle the rest."

They shook hands again and Kade headed back to his car. As soon he as he pulled away he called his twin sister. "Kenzi, I know everyone is gearing up for the wedding in a couple days, but I need some advice on how to make something special happen." Without attempting to pretty it up, he gave Kenzi an overview of the state of his relationship with Annie—right up to her saying she didn't believe he loved her. "I don't blame her for doubting me, Kenzi, but I'm not about to give up on us. I will prove to her what I'm feeling isn't new. She's always been the one for me. This will represent a fresh start for us, a chance to get it right. No one I know could get Forever fixed and returned on the timetable I need. Show me how to flex my Barrington muscle."

Kenzi laughed. "Barrington muscle? Asher would love that. But if you're looking for someone who can have it done without fanfare, I'll ask Dax."

"I want to be the one who makes it happen. I just need a little direction."

"Piece of advice?"

"Sure."

"Your brothers are climbing the walls here. They need something to do. Involving them in whatever you're planning would make them feel like you need them. They talk shit a lot, but in the end they're just little boys who want to know they matter."

"I don't want to lose control of this. This is about Annie and showing her how I feel."

"Well, think about it."

Kade groaned. "I don't want this to be a circus. All I need is the helicopter refurbished and back by the wedding." He could almost see Kenzi's pleading eyes. "Okay, I'll ask Asher and the others for their help. But Clay is not part of this, nor are Viviana's brothers. I'm serious."

Chapter Nineteen

SATURDAY MORNING ANNIE did her makeup in the mirror. Somehow she'd made it through the longest few days at work ever. She was exhausted from the extra trips she'd scheduled herself for and sore from the crazy amount of time she'd spent on her treadmill. As she dressed, she discovered a perk of a week of high stress that involved no sugar—the outfit she'd purchased for the Barrington wedding was a whole lot looser.

Yes, she had decided to not attend the Barrington wedding, but then she'd made the mistake of telling Claire. Her friend had not only offered to go with her, but had told Annie that she owed it to herself to be there. She'd claimed she needed closure, and Annie had argued she'd just endured a week of that.

What had finally won Annie over was Claire saying, "Do you really want your goodbye to Kade to be an angry one? After everything you've been to each other, don't you owe yourself better?"

Annie did regret the way she'd stormed away from Kade when he'd come to her office. She didn't want him hurting any more than she wanted that for herself. Annie's decision to go had quickly been followed by a mild panic regarding what she would wear and what the heck to give a billionaire couple for a wedding present. Thankfully, Claire was a source of advice for that as well. The knee-length light-blue linen dress was casual but chic, perfect for what promised to be a family-and-close-friends wedding. Claire suggested a personalized gift. With that in mind, working with her father, Annie came up with a recipe for a light ale and produced a case of it. She was particularly proud of the label she'd designed for it: G&V Ale. The small print included instructions for celebrating with it post-baby birth. It was adorable and had already been delivered to the lodge. Easy.

Annie glanced at the clock on the wall. Claire was late, which was uncharacteristic for her. She also didn't answer when Annie tried to call to confirm she was on her way.

Annie sent Claire a follow-up text asking her to call as soon as she received the message. She gathered her handbag and tried to ring Claire one more time.

Nothing.

Just then she received a text from Will asking her if she could drop by the office before the wedding. She was the type to arrive to events early because she hated to be late. Technically she did have time, but not much.

Is it an emergency?
Will: **I wouldn't ask if it weren't important.**

That was definitely the truth. She sent a text to Claire instructing her to meet her at the lodge then wrote to Will:
On my way.

Ten minutes later she pulled into the parking lot of her

office and smoothed her dress down, taking a deep breath as she did. Dealing with the unexpected was par for the course when one owned their own company. Whatever it was, she'd handle as much of it as she could immediately then come back to sort it out after the wedding.

As she exited her car, it was Claire rather than Will who waved to her from the hangar door. Annie shook her head, confused. She walked toward her, wondering if Claire had asked to meet her there and she'd somehow forgotten. No, Claire had said she wanted to see her family while she was in town so she'd flown in the night before. They hadn't spoken again after that, but the plan had definitely been to meet at Annie's.

The sound of a helicopter approaching drew Annie's attention to the sky. Like a mother knows the footsteps of her own child, she recognized the sound of Forever before the small craft appeared over the treetops.

What the hell?

Freshly painted silver with her name in black lettering on the side, she temporarily stole Annie's ability to breathe. It had broken Annie's heart the morning she'd come to work and the craft was gone, but she'd told herself it was for the best. She couldn't hate Will for scrapping the chopper, considering she'd told him to. But there she was—back and better than before. How?

As soon as the helicopter touched down, the engine cut and Will exited it. He walked to where Annie was standing in stunned silence.

"At least listen to what he has to say," Will said, then

walked past Annie.

Annie looked over her shoulder to see Claire filming with her phone. She motioned for Annie to turn back toward the helicopter.

Feeling as if everything were moving in slow motion, Annie did. Kade was standing beside the open passenger side door with a smile that warmed her right down to her toes.

He took a step toward her.

She took a step toward him.

They met in the middle and simply stood there for a long moment, staring into each other's eyes. In a husky voice, he asked, "What do you think of Forever now?"

Was that what he was offering or was he referring to her helicopter? She physically shook from the intensity of her conflicting emotions. She wanted to throw her arms around him even as she fought an equally strong desire to run before she made a fool of herself again. This could simply be an extravagant parting gift.

He took both of her hands in his. "You have every reason to doubt me, Annie. It took having my life turned upside down for me to realize you were always meant to be part of it."

The rest of the world faded away, unimportant. There was only Kade and her fear.

"I love you, Annie."

All she could do was look back at him and hope her nervously churning stomach didn't empty itself. He deserved the truth, though. "I'm scared, Kade."

"I'm scared too," he said, pulling her into his arms. "Terrified that my thick-headedness cost me my chance with you. No one else ever touched my heart, Annie, because it has always been yours. Sappy as it may sound, I gave it to you our second year of school. You'd spilled milk . . ."

Her fears fell away because the love in his eyes could not be questioned. Annie burst into tears as a huge smile spread across her face. "And you offered me your Vegemite sandwich. That's the day I fell in love with you too." *He loves me. This is really happening.*

He hugged her to his chest, tucking her beneath his chin. His heart beat so loudly that she knew he was feeling the same level of emotion. "I'm so sorry I left you, Annie."

She sniffed. "You had to go. I knew it then. You needed to take care of your family."

He raised his head. "I did, but I should have taken you with me." He nodded toward her helicopter. "I hope you're not upset with me for going behind your back to fix her up. I knew how much she meant to you. I also knew you had plans to refurbish her. You made sensible choices that built up your company. We both put what we wanted on hold because we had responsibilities we felt needed to come first, but doing the right thing shouldn't cost us what we love."

"No, it shouldn't. What you did with Forever is amazing. I don't know what to say beyond thank you." She wiped the tears from her eyes. With the two possible paths her life could have taken laid out before her, she saw their time apart in a new light. Who would she have been had she gone with him to Wabonga? "Maybe we needed that time. Back then I loved you in a way that left no room for me. My dreams were whatever I thought you would want from me. When you left I was forced to ask myself what I wanted. I took the best of what I learned while I was with you and became my own person."

He cupped a side of her face with one of his hands. "You certainly did. I want a second chance at forever with you and I hope that this"—he referenced the helicopter behind him—"represents a new beginning for both of us. We belong together, just like she belongs in your hangar." With no regard for the suit he wore, he dropped to one knee and held out a green diamond ring. "I've loved you my whole life. It took me a while to see it, but a part of me always knew this moment would happen for us. Say you'll marry me, Annie. Two crazy second graders couldn't be wrong about something this important."

"Oh, my gosh, Kade, it's so. . ." She hesitated. *Huge. Expensive.* "Where did you get the ring?"

"Sophie gave it to me. Dale bought it for her as a token of a new beginning for them. She thought it was fitting for us."

A new beginning. It was fitting. "You've gotten pretty close to them, haven't you?" *Close enough to leave with them?* She didn't dare ask.

"Absolutely."

The little voice in her head that had whispered he might not feel this way when his life settled reared its ugly head again, but as she looked at the stunning ring she realized her happiness was truly in her own hands. Every single time her helicopter lifted off the ground, she had to trust it wouldn't fail her. One day it might, but she would never leave the ground if she let the fear of what could go wrong stop her from soaring through the skies.

And what a sad life that would be.

She held out her left hand. "Hell yes, I'll marry you, Kade. For me, it has always been you."

He slid the diamond on her finger and stood. "I don't know where this crazy Barrington/Thompson thing will take me, but I know I want you by my side. Will you come along on this crazy ride?"

Nodding wildly, she threw herself into his arms and kissed him with all the boldness of a woman who knew she was loved. He kissed her back with all the possessiveness of a man laying claim to what was his. When they finally broke off the kiss, they were both breathing heavily and chuckling.

"I love you, Kade Thompson," she said, running her fingers over his firm lips. "I just hope Kent is as good in bed."

He gave her a playful swat on the arse. "Is that what you're thinking about right now?"

Lighthearted, she shrugged and shifted against his cock, loving how hard he was for her. "Sorry, you're not?"

He kissed her deeply until she almost forgot they had an audience. She glanced back only to find they were alone. "Where did they go?"

Between kisses Kade said, "I asked Will to drive Claire to the lodge." He swung her up into his arms. "Do you still have that big leather couch in your office?"

"Yes," Annie said breathlessly. "But we can't miss the wedding."

He strode through the hangar toward her office. "I had them push it back an hour."

"You didn't." Annie blushed bright red.

"Too little time? Should I call and ask for more?" he asked as he pushed the door of her office open and closed it behind them. The grin on his face was sexy as hell.

"Don't you dare," she scolded, but she was laughing. All embarrassment fell away when her dress hit the floor. An hour? They could make that work.

"Oh, I dare." He unbuttoned his shirt and threw it on the floor. He pulled his phone out of his pocket, put on a cheesy romance song, and continued to strip to the music. When he was naked with his cock at full attention, he helped her out of her lingerie, and twirled her around in a dance that left them both laughing.

While bent over his arm in a final dip, he trailed kisses across her shoulder and began to adore her breasts with his lips and tongue. The nature of the dance changed as hunger for each other took over.

A SHORT TIME later, after nearly being late to the wedding and arriving looking both flustered and sated, Kade and Annie held hands as they watched Grant and Viviana exchange their vows. It was a remarkably simple yet tasteful ceremony, attended by the family and a few close friends. Annie's family was in attendance as well as Pamela and Dave.

The newlyweds had their first dance then cut their cake, because Viviana had joked that the last thing a pregnant bride should have to do on her wedding day was wait for the cake. No one argued with that.

Everyone was seated beneath a white tent when Grant stood and tapped a fork against his glass, drawing the attention of all. He smiled at Viviana before speaking. "If someone had told me that Viv and I would marry in Australia with all of you in attendance, I wouldn't have believed them. Yet, here we are. Our family and friendships have been tested, but we came out better and stronger because of it. The road before us may still hold challenges, but we've proven that together we can handle anything." He looked at his new wife again and then around the room. "I used to watch the families on TV and wonder why ours didn't get along the way theirs did. Over the years, I've realized it's because they weren't real."

"I'm serious." In response to a round of chuckles, Grant raised his hand in a quiet request for another moment of their time. "Viviana, for better or for worse, you're now a Barrington. God knows our family needs—"

"And we're happy to have her." Dale stood, and clapped Grant on the back as he spoke over him.

Lance chimed in. "Good save, Dad."

Viviana started laughing. Sophie shook her head, but she was smiling.

"I don't get what's so funny," Connor grumbled.

Dylan socked his brother in the arm. "You don't remember how he used to insult her?"

"What's funny about him being a dick?" Although Connor had likely meant the question solely for his brother's ears, it was heard by most of the group.

Viviana's father moved to stand behind his sons and bent to tell them to quiet or he'd tan their hides.

Grant interjected, "I was merely expressing how good you are for my family, Viviana."

Viviana rose to her feet and gave her husband a kiss. "I know. I don't know that I'd want you to change, even if you could."

Still looking concerned, Grant said, "Even when I first said it, I never meant—"

"Stop while you're ahead, Grant," Asher advised.

With flushed cheeks, Grant did. He simply gathered his wife to him and kissed her until she looked as flustered as he did.

It was a sweet, romantic display no one seemed to mind. Kade's attention swung to Annie who was smiling in her seat beside him. "I want to announce our news, but I don't want to take away from their day."

Annie ran a hand down his jaw. "So many people wouldn't think like that, but it doesn't surprise me at all that you do." She glanced around, down at her ring, then smiled back up at him. "They all probably know, anyway."

He laid his hand over hers. "I spoke to Grant earlier, and he said they're heading to Boston tomorrow night. They asked me if I'd go back with them."

Her eyes rounded. "What did you say?"

"I said I needed to talk to you about it first. I know your business is important to you, Annie, but could you run it from Boston for a while?"

She searched his face before answering. "I could."

"You said something earlier that hit home to me. I don't want you to ever put your dreams aside for mine. That's not what love requires. You've always been one step ahead of me when it comes to planning. Help me do this right. I'm ridiculously, crazy rich, but I need to do something of importance with my inheritance. There has to be a reason that money came to me. I don't know what that is yet, but I'm confident we can figure it out together and do something that will make a real difference to people in need."

She shook her head in bemusement. "You are one amazing man, Kade."

To make her laugh, he puffed out his chest and said, "*I am* pretty wonderful. When something is this good, you should seal the deal fast. What do you think of having our wedding next week?"

She slapped a hand on his chest and gasped. "Next week? Where? Here? In Boston?"

He nuzzled her neck. "Wherever we are."

She chuckled. "What about my parents? Harrison? Claire?"

"We'll fly them over. Money doesn't solve everything, but it does make planning easy. I'm pretty sure I can snap my fingers and have a fleet of private planes in the air."

Annie shook him by the shoulders. "Oh, boy, you do need my help. Someone needs to keep your feet grounded in reality."

He tapped her chin lightly. "Then what do you say to a quick wedding?"

She nodded. "And it would save us from whatever Clay

would have planned."

"Oh, shit, I almost forgot about that." He shuddered.

The band began to play a slow ballad. Kade stood and took Annie by the hand. He spun her onto the floor and into his arms. They still had a lot to figure out, but none of it mattered at that moment. They were both where they were always meant to be.

Epilogue

A FEW MONTHS later, in a park just outside Boston, Annie waved nervously at a crowd of people who had gathered along the path. The click-clack of the horses' shoes hitting pavement was nearly drowned out by the applause. Never had Annie imagined her wedding day would include a custom-made designer dress, a tiara worth more than her fleet of helicopters, white doves, an ornate white horse-drawn carriage, and nearly a thousand people.

With his arm resting on the back of the carriage seat behind her, Kade leaned in to wave with her and asked, "Do you feel like a princess?"

"Would that make you Prince Charming?" Annie smiled. Unlike the extravagance of the day, this was the part of her wedding day she'd dreamed about—Kade at her side looking at her the same way she looked at him.

Kade winked. "Hardly. What did that guy ever do besides show up? I also suspect he was horrible in the sack. Wasn't he with Cinderella, Sleeping Beauty, and Snow White? There must have been a reason none of them kept him around."

Annie laughed. "You have put a disturbing amount of thought into this."

With a surprisingly serious expression, Kade answered, "I have. You don't need a Prince Charming, Annie. You're not a damsel in distress waiting for some man to sweep in and save you. If anything, I think I need you a hell of a lot more than you need me. You have a way of bringing out the best in people—even in the most awkward situations. The Andrades are here today because you made them feel welcome."

"I had no idea how many of them there were," Annie joked, then added gently, "Plus they were victims of Patrice's jealousy just as much as you were. Julia, Gio's wife, told me how Patrice used her own sons as pawns in a sick game of revenge no one understood until just before she died. It's such a sad story. That's why I agreed to all of this"—she waved from the carriage at the crowd—"because your uncle Alessandro said they needed to celebrate your return. They needed closure."

Kade kissed her cheek. "Alessandro is quite a character. I don't believe everyone here is actually related to him."

Still waving at the people they passed, Annie said, "Sophie said he has a flexible definition of family, one that doesn't require blood relation. Just love."

Kade nuzzled her again. "I like that definition of family."

"I do too."

"Look at that," Kade said while pointing to the sky. "Is someone skywriting our names in a heart?"

A quick look confirmed that Kade's guess was correct.

Annie chuckled. "Clay went a little overboard, don't you think?"

"Dax said he's never seen Clay put so much thought into a project. I'm almost afraid to see what he has planned for the reception." Kade wiggled his eyebrows. "A trapeze act? Really, it's kind of cool to have no idea."

"Or hot-air balloon races?" There was no limit to what Clay was capable of. When it came to the wedding, it had been like having a real-life fairy godmother—if one replaced the fairy's wand with a bottomless bank account. Leaning back into the warmth of Kade's embrace, Annie sighed in happy contentment. Yes, that day was a wild adventure, but with Kade at her side her life would probably be full of those. "I'm so happy Viviana was able to make it today with her due date so close. She looks calmer than Grant, though."

"About that," Kade said, looking serious again. "Do you mind if we postpone our honeymoon until after the baby is born? I'd like to be here for the baby's birth."

"Of course. We probably should stick around anyway, because Andrew said he and Helene want to make it official soon as well. He didn't say it, but I think he needed to resolve things with you before he could move forward with her."

"I think you're right. And I wouldn't want to miss that wedding, either."

Family had always been a priority to Kade, and it was heartwarming to see that despite everything else that had changed—he hadn't. He'd made sure Pamela and Dave, as well as Annie's parents, were just as much a part of the wedding as Sophie and Dale. When Kade loved, he did so with thoughtfulness and unmatched loyalty. He'd be a good husband, an amazing father to their children, and with unsurprising ease, was already learning to straddle his two worlds. He was changing the focus of his tour company to search and rescue support and training. They were starting in Wabonga as well as Bright, with plans of expanding across Australia. Volunteers would not only receive the best equipment and training, they'd be compensated for any income they lost at work during rescue missions. Kade had been prepared to fund the entire project himself, but as soon as the story had broken, donors began to line up to be part of it.

Ah, the power of the Barrington name.

Annie was making changes as well. Her company was already expanding to include a line of private jets for international commuters, and Kade had purchased a building in Boston for her satellite office. Another man might have suggested that Annie didn't need to work anymore, but Kade understood how much her company meant to her.

Love wasn't about having to choose.

Just before the carriage stopped, they passed a line of their immediate family. Everyone was smiling and waving—everyone except Ian. Annie gave Kade's hand a squeeze when she saw his expression change as he noticed a lack of enthusiasm from that particular brother.

"He'll come around," Annie assured him.

Kade nodded once, then his smile returned. "Alessandro says love heals all wounds." He kissed her gently on the lips.

"I can't argue that. Do we know anyone with the balls to take him on?"

Annie was momentarily lost in the sensation of his lips once again grazing over hers. When he raised his head and her ability to think coherently began to return, she snapped her fingers and said, "Claire!"

As Kade helped Annie out of the carriage, he glanced from her friend to his brother and back. "She'd definitely call him on his shit."

Annie clapped her hands together. "Are you up for a little matchmaking, Kade?"

"I can't imagine Ian would want me to get involved with his private life." A slow smile spread across his face. "Let's do it."

Annie followed her heart and kissed him soundly, not caring they had an audience. "Do you know how much I love you, Kade Thompson-Barrington?"

He swung her around, kissing her deeply and getting himself tangled up in her train. "Can't be as much as I love you, Mrs. Annie Thompson-Barrington."

With a blush, Annie looked around and confessed, "Is it wrong I'm enjoying today? I mean, I would have been happy with anything. I know the whole fairy tale huge wedding is over the top, but it's also . . ." She struggled for how to put it into words. After a lifetime of thinking the day would never happen, having it be so magical somehow fit.

"Somehow right," he finished, knowing her almost better than she knew herself. "We've worked hard, Annie. We've made sensible, good choices, and always tried to do for others before we did for ourselves. No, life isn't a fairy tale, but if we do it right, it might be better than one."

In the circle of his arms, surrounded by family and friends, she said, "Amen to that," and hugged him tightly. He hugged her back with the same intensity.

No, theirs had not been the easiest of roads, but if she could go back and do it all over—she'd want it to turn out the same way.

They were lovers as well as best friends.

And they had their forever now.

THE END

Not ready to say good-bye to these characters? Sign up for my newsletter via my website www.ruthcardello.com and stay informed about releases.

Never Good-bye will be the next book in this series and is expected to release early 2019.

Made in the USA
Monee, IL
20 August 2021